"Get inside the house n

"What's happening?" Sabrina asked.

"Men with guns." Jake peeked out the front window and saw the car speed up to the front of the house, and then two men with guns leaned out and started firing.

"Get down!" he shouted. Robby, still in her arms, started crying.

The bullets kept coming. He pressed them both toward the back of the house, but he still had a clear view of the front window. The men were getting out and approaching the house.

Robby cried and Sabrina did her best to comfort him and keep him quiet.

"What's happening?" she demanded.

"Creed put a hit out on you. His suppliers want you out of the picture."

She clutched Robby, and he could see that news shook her.

"What are they doing?"

"They're approaching the house. Do you have a safe room or any other way out of here?"

She shook her head. "The backyard is gated. We'd have to climb over it, and my neighbor has a big, mean dog."

They were trapped.

Virginia Vaughan is a born-and-raised Mississippi girl. She is blessed to come from a large Southern family, and her fondest memories include listening to stories recounted around the dinner table. She was a lover of books from a young age, devouring tales of romance, danger and love. She soon started writing them herself. You can connect with Virginia through her website, virginiavaughanonline.com, or through the publisher.

Books by Virginia Vaughan

Love Inspired Suspense

Lone Star Defenders

Dangerous Christmas Investigation

Cowboy Protectors

Kidnapped in Texas
Texas Ranch Target
Dangerous Texas Hideout
Texas Ranch Cold Case

Cowboy Lawmen

Texas Twin Abduction
Texas Holiday Hideout
Texas Target Standoff
Texas Baby Cover-Up
Texas Killer Connection
Texas Buried Secrets

Visit the Author Profile page
at LoveInspired.com for more titles.

Dangerous
Christmas
Investigation

VIRGINIA VAUGHAN

Love INSPIRED SUSPENSE
INSPIRATIONAL ROMANCE

LOVE INSPIRED® SUSPENSE
INSPIRATIONAL ROMANCE

ISBN-13: 978-1-335-48395-9

Dangerous Christmas Investigation

Copyright © 2024 by Virginia Vaughan

Love Inspired
22 Adelaide St. West, 41st Floor
Toronto, Ontario M5H 4E3, Canada
www.LoveInspired.com

Printed in U.S.A.

And I will restore to you the years that the locust hath eaten, the cankerworm, and the caterpiller, and the palmerworm, my great army which I sent among you.
—*Joel* 2:25

To Carter. Your adventurous spirit inspires me to try new things. You always have a smile on your face and laughter in your heart. Your kind and loving spirit makes me so proud of the person you are becoming.

ONE

Deputy Sabrina Reagan hummed along to a Christmas song playing on the radio as she waited at the stoplight to make a left-hand turn into the shopping center parking lot. A chill had settled in the December air and, for the first time in years, she was looking forward to the approaching holiday. Christmas decorations had sprung up everywhere she looked. The light poles that lined the streets had been adorned with flags reading Merry Christmas or Happy Holidays at each intersection, the radio station played Christmas songs on a loop and a twenty-foot Christmas tree had been erected in court square of their little Texas town. She'd promised her son,

Robby, that they would go to the lighting ceremony this weekend and she was looking forward to seeing the smile on his little face at all the lights and wonder of the season. It had been a long time since she'd looked forward to Christmas but this year, finally, she was, and Robby had a lot to do with it.

A horn honked behind her and she realized she had the turn arrow. She waved to the offended driver then made her left turn. She'd been lost in thought about Christmas again. This was the first year that Robby was really old enough to understand what was happening—as much as a four-year-old could understand. She glanced in her rearview mirror and adjusted it to see him sleeping in his car seat on the back seat. The Christmas party at his preschool had worn him out. When she'd picked him up, he'd run to her with pictures he'd drawn, crafts he'd made and a secret present for her inside a paper sack that he'd forbidden her to peek at.

She thought of her brother, Robby's namesake, and how much he would have loved seeing his nephew's eyes sparkle at all the Christmas lights. She was determined to make this Christmas a good one. They were due. Her brother's death five years ago had shattered her peace and turned Sabrina's life upside down. She was finally, slowly climbing out of a spiral of grief and her little boy had been the one to give her the will to want to live again.

She pulled into a parking space in front of the grocery store and glanced at Robby's face as he slept. Despite his name, it wasn't her brother's face she saw reflected in the features and mop of dark hair.

Jake.

She'd clung to Robby as her lifeline after her brother's death and discovering her pregnancy, but it had been Robby's father that she had pushed away in her grief.

She cut the engine and sighed.

Yes, she'd pushed Jake away, but he'd been the one to leave town. He hadn't fought hard enough or stuck around long enough to even discover he'd had a son. And he'd never responded to the letter she'd mailed to him letting him know about the birth of their little boy.

Why then did her heart still break at the idea of never seeing him again?

She shoved those thoughts aside and turned her attention back to the present. Her mother had always told her not to wake a sleeping child but she'd neglected to place a grocery order and there wasn't enough food at her house to feed the little guy tonight. She had to wake him and make a grocery run. From experience, she knew he would be cranky. He was worn out from his long, busy day.

She climbed out of the vehicle and had barely closed her own door before a man appeared from behind a parked car and pressed her against her SUV. He produced a knife and stuck it at her throat, digging it into her skin.

All of her police training meant nothing in the moment. Sabrina's heart raced and her knees threatened to buckle at the fear that pulsed through her. She stared into her attacker's face. He was young but there was a coldness behind his gray eyes. He could end her life with one move and she sensed no hesitation from him.

She gulped down several heavy breaths then dared a glance at her baby. She could only see the top of his head but he seemed to be still sleeping soundly and her fear morphed into anger. If this was a carjacking, he could have it but he wouldn't leave here with her child inside.

"Mr. Creed says you've been sticking your nose where it doesn't belong." The man's sneer was only accentuated by his hot, sticky breath.

Creed. So this wasn't a carjacking but that didn't make this assailant any less dangerous.

"Who are you?"

"I'm here to deliver a message. Back off unless you want us coming after someone you love."

Her instinct was to fight back but fear paralyzed her as she followed his gaze to the back seat. Her cheeks burned with anger and her body tensed. She couldn't allow anything to happen to her son.

He must have felt her fight reflex kick in because he released her and was gone, disappearing behind another row of cars before Sabrina could even catch her breath.

Her gun was still at her side in its holster but she hadn't even had time to try to reach for it. At least he hadn't taken it from her. That was brave. He'd known he had the upper hand threatening her son.

She crawled back into her SUV and locked the doors. Her hands were shaking with a mixture of fear and rage boiling through her veins. She gripped the steering wheel, trying to calm down enough to think straight.

Creed had threatened her son.

Paul Creed was a drug dealer who'd gotten too big for his britches and fancied himself some kind of drug kingpin. Sabrina had targeted him right away when she'd started working Narcotics at the Mercy County Sheriff's Office. She blamed Creed for her brother's overdose and, while many longed to make detective or move up to Homicide, Sabrina was happy to remain where she was. She wasn't going anywhere until Paul Creed was behind bars once and for all.

She started the SUV and sped away and didn't stop until she was out of the shopping center parking lot. She hit the speed dial on her cell phone and waited until her supervisor, Commander Kent Morgan, picked up.

She gave him a quick rundown of the incident.

"Are you or Robby hurt?"

She liked that that was his main concern. He was only ten years or so older than her with a wife and a kid on the way but he'd become a fatherly figure to her and tough but caring supervisor. "No, we're both fine. I'm shaken but Robby slept through it all."

"Good. I'll call over to the security office at the plaza and get copies of the security tapes. Maybe we can identify this assailant."

She hoped so. She would enjoy putting a little fear into this kid the way he had her, though she doubted he would roll over and admit to being ordered to threaten her by Paul Creed. Creed had a way of keeping his employees loyal.

"Have you heard from Max?" Max Harris, a DEA agent who'd gone undercover in Creed's group, had vanished from town several weeks ago. At first, she'd worried that Creed had discovered his identity and harmed him, but a call from his DEA supervisor had let them know that he was safe and would be returning soon. He hadn't given a reason for Max's absence but she'd been glad for some kind of update. She and Max had committed to working together to find evidence to identify Creed's supplier and end his organization. He was usually the one to give her a heads-up when she'd been targeted but his absence meant she hadn't been privy to this attack. She didn't like the feeling of being ambushed and was ready for Max to return and keep her up to date on what was happening in Creed's organization. Plus, she was curious to know what had caused him to leave so abruptly.

"I haven't seen him yet but I received a call saying he was back in town and would meet me here at the sheriff's office in an hour."

That was a relief. "I'll be there too.

First, I need to drop Robby off at my mother's."

"That's a good idea. Stay safe."

She ended the call, glad to hear Max had finally returned. She was ready to have Paul Creed behind bars and she couldn't make that happen without him.

She ran through a fast food drive-through and ordered Robby chicken nuggets and fries, then turned the car toward her mother's house. It wasn't the nutritious meal he should have had but it would have to do for tonight.

Twenty minutes later, she pulled up to her mother's house, parked then unbuckled her son from his car seat. Her mother met her at the front door.

"Sabrina, I didn't know you were coming by tonight."

"Neither did I," she explained. She went inside and set Robby down in front of the television. She gave him his nuggets and fries, turned on his favorite cartoon, and he was a happy kid. Sabrina pulled her mother into the kitchen and recounted what had happened. "Can I leave Robby here for a couple of hours? I need to go meet Kent at the sheriff's office."

"Of course you can. I'm supposed to meet Bob at ten tonight. Do you think you'll be back before then?"

"10:00 p.m.?" Her mother's new boy-friend, Bob Crawford, kept odd hours. "I should be back before that but why so late?"

She shrugged. "He has meetings all evening but he wants us to drive to that new resort in Houston for the weekend. I can cancel if you need me to keep Robby longer," she offered.

Her mother liked this new beau and Sabrina didn't want to do anything to hamper her burgeoning relationship. Besides, she would feel better having Robby with her and ensuring his safety for herself. "Don't cancel. Enjoy the weekend. I'll be back for Robby in plenty of time before you leave."

"Okay, but be careful. I don't like how you keep placing yourself in danger this way, Sabrina."

Her mother worried about her and that was understandable but she of all people knew the reason why Sabrina was so committed to bringing Paul Creed's organization down. Sabrina had lost a brother but her mother had lost a son.

"I know you worry, Mom, but I have to do this."

"I wish you'd become a teacher or an accountant or something safe like that."

She chuckled that her mom thought teaching was a safe profession but didn't say so. Instead, she pulled her into a hug. "I'll be okay. I'm just heading to the sheriff's office to meet up with Kent and an informant. I'll only be an hour or two."

She kissed Robby's cheek and told him to mind his grandma before she ran out the door and turned her SUV toward the sheriff's office.

The parking lot wasn't full, as the day shift had left and only a skeleton crew worked the evening shift at the office while the remaining deputies were out on patrol. She parked then headed into the office, waving at her fellow deputies Mike Tyner and Drake Shaw. The evening dispatcher, Allison Meeks, was in a small room in the corner. Sabrina waved to her as she passed by and Allison returned her wave.

"Have you seen Kent?" she asked Drake and Mike.

"I think he's in the break room," Drake told her. "I saw him head back that way a while ago."

She hurried back there and found Kent pounding on the vending machine. A pack of peanut M&M's fell to the bottom and he bent down and fished it out. He tore into it and popped one into his mouth as he looked at her.

"Are you okay?"

She took a deep breath. "I will be. I think I was more angry than frightened especially since Robby was there with me."

"I get that."

"Where's Max? Have you seen him?"

He nodded. "He came in the back entrance a few minutes ago. He was using my office to make a call."

"I think I'll go see him and tell him what happened. He's going to be furious but I'm so glad he's back."

It wasn't unusual for informants to enter through the back entrance to avoid being seen by everyone inside the sheriff's office. Of course, she trusted her coworkers but it never hurt to be cautious. Max's work with the DEA had to remain a secret in order to protect his undercover identity.

She walked down the back hallway and spotted a tall figure coming out of Kent's office. She recognized the broad shoulders and the dark hair. "Max!"

He turned and his mouth twitched, a tic she had never seen in Max before. She'd only seen it from...

Sabrina's heart stopped cold.

This man was not Max.

It was Jake. Max's twin and her ex.

"Jake! What are you doing here?"

Shock rattled through him at her recognition. He grabbed her arm and pulled her into the office, closing the door behind him.

"Sabrina, how did you know it was me?" he asked before immediately waving away the question. She'd always been one of the few people that could tell him and Max apart. Even their own father couldn't but that could have been caused by either the excessive drinking or the apathy about his sons' lives. Their mother had been the only one before she died, then Sabrina. To everyone else, he and his brother had been identical.

He should have known he wouldn't be able to fool Sabrina but he honestly hadn't even expected to see her. He'd forgotten how beautiful she was. Her shoulder-length dark hair was pulled into a bun at the nape of her neck and her green eyes were wide with surprise. He glanced at the uniform she wore complete with badge on her shirt and gun at her hip. She was a deputy. Max had failed to mention that or that she was his liaison to the Mercy County Sheriff's Office. That would have been nice to know. His brother had spoken about his undercover work in Mercy and many of the details but Jake wasn't surprised he hadn't mentioned Sabrina to him. They didn't speak of her often, not after the way things had ended between her and Jake five years earlier.

He'd fallen in love with this dark-haired beauty but her brother's death had sent her spiraling into grief. Try as he might, he hadn't been able to pull her out of it. It had broken his heart not to be able to help her through it. She'd pushed him away so many times he'd felt he had no choice but to leave her to her grief. He'd regretted it every day since.

She folded her arms and glared at him. "What are you doing here, Jake? And where is Max?" Realization dawned on her. "Are you trying to fool people into believing you're Max?"

He was, but he certainly hadn't been expecting to be called out on it. "Why not? There aren't many people who can tell us apart."

"I did."

"Well sure, you can, but who else could?"

"Why are you doing this? Where is Max? Why isn't he here?"

He saw her look of anticipation and knew the news he had to tell her was going to be difficult. He did his best to keep his own emotions in check but it wasn't easy. Apparently, she and Max had grown close during their investigation into Paul Creed.

He pulled out a chair for her. "Maybe you should sit down."

Her eyes widened and the annoyance on her face turned to worry, but she took the seat. "What's wrong? Where is Max?"

He took a deep breath, then just spilled it. "Max and I met up a few weeks ago. I'd gotten some intel from an informant about movement by a drug cartel that I thought he might want to know. We met halfway and I gave him what I had. We hadn't seen one another in a while so we spent a few hours catching up. We were driving to a diner when the car slid on some ice and went off the road. I woke up in the hospital with a concussion, a broken wrist—" he held up a cast on his left arm as proof "—and some cuts and bruises but otherwise I was fine. Max, on the other hand, wasn't. He'd sustained major head injuries and was brain-dead. His DEA supervisor, Carl Price, was called in and was there at the hospital with me waiting for the end. We talked a good bit about Max and about the mission. That's when we came up with this plan. I wanted a way to honor my brother's legacy and finishing his last assignment was a way I could do that. We're both law enforcement. I've been with San Antonio PD for four years and this isn't the first time I've worked undercover. Carl got the okay from his higher-ups then filled me in on the basics of the case and the major players and I figured I could bluff my way through the rest."

She shook her head. "This can't be real. How was this even authorized?"

"That should tell you how important it is to them to find Creed's supplier that they gave us the okay. I have to at least try for Max."

Tears had filled her eyes as he re-counted the story and now a few slipped down her cheek. She put her hands over her face. He hadn't realized how close she and Max had been and that surprised him. Max knew how much Jake had loved her and how hard it had been for him to leave her. He'd also known how futile it would have been to stay.

Jake was glad to see she'd finally been able to move past her grief and pull her life together but the last thing he'd expected was for her to take a job at the sheriff's office.

She wiped her face with her hand. "Poor Max. He was a good man."

"Yes, he was." Jake hadn't yet properly dealt with his feelings. There hadn't been time because he'd been dealing with preparing to step into his place. He took a chance and reached for her hands. At first, she accepted his touch but then she slowly pulled them away.

"Sabrina, I know you want to get this guy Paul Creed as much as I do. Do you want this investigation to implode because Max died?"

She shook her head. "I want Creed in jail."

"I can do this. Max's boss told me all about his investigation into Creed. I know you have your reason for wanting to bring him down." While he was surprised that she'd joined the sheriff's office, he wasn't surprised she'd chosen the narcotics division. He didn't mention her brother. He didn't need to. "I have a reason as well. I can do this but I need you to be on my side. Can you do that?"

She stood and paced the floor. "Does Kent know about this?"

"No. He didn't even flinch when he saw me. Only Max's DEA supervisor and now you know."

"You're asking me to lie to my entire team."

"Isn't that what undercover work is about? I'm only asking you not to out me as Jake. Let me honor my brother."

He thought for a moment she was going to refuse but, after wrestling with it for several moments, she finally nodded. "I'm only going along with this because I don't want Max's investigation to have been in vain but I'm worried, Jake. I don't know if you can pull this off."

"I can," he assured her. He wanted to see confidence in her green eyes but all he saw was doubt in them. About him. About if he could complete this mission and take down a notorious drug dealer.

He had to do it. He owed it to his brother's memory to finish what he'd started.

He owed it to her too.

Jake still had a difficult time believing that he was sitting in a room with Sabrina Reagan. She looked good. The last time he'd seen her, she'd been an emotional wreck with grief after her brother's death. She'd been angry and bitter and nothing he could do or say had made it better. He'd wanted to be with her, to give her comfort during such a difficult time, but she'd pushed him away.

The way he'd left her still broke his heart. It had felt brutal to leave town while she was still struggling but there hadn't been much he could have done for her. They'd planned to leave town together and he'd already had a job lined up in Dallas but it hadn't been a good fit for him. She was supposed to have come with him. That had been the plan. Only her brother's death had changed everything.

He was glad to have her on his side again but things still felt awkward between them.

"Sabrina, do we need to talk about how things ended with us?"

She stiffened at his suggestion and her chin jutted out. "Not at all. That was a long time ago, Jake. That's all in the past."

He nodded and breathed a sigh of relief. "I'm glad to hear that." He pulled out a chair and motioned for her to sit down again. He took the opposite chair. "Why don't you give me a rundown of the case you and Max were trying to build against Creed."

"I thought you said Max's boss filled you in."

"He did but I know how undercover work flows. I'm sure there's stuff Max hadn't gotten around to reporting yet. I figured you would be the closest to him in that respect. I'm also interested in how you became his liaison."

"I joined the sheriff's office after my brother died. As you know, my father was in law enforcement and so was his father. It's a family tradition. I guess they always hoped that Robby would join the force but he never wanted that, even before the drugs took him. After his overdose, I asked to work Narcotics. As long as those drugs are on the street, other people's family members are in danger."

"How did the DEA get involved?"

"Your brother was investigating a smuggling ring that he believed was supplying local drug dealers. He was trying to connect Paul Creed to this ring. That was his primary mission. He wanted to find out who was supplying him with drugs then follow that back to the supplier. He believed it was someone working out of this part of Texas. He discovered I had been targeting members of Creed's group and had arrested many of them so his boss reached out to the sheriff. They informed us that he was going to be working undercover in town. The plan was that I would be his contact and whatever information he gathered, I would send to his boss at the DEA. Imagine my surprise when I learned Max was the undercover agent on the case. It was unsettling."

"I imagine it was."

She stared at him then looked away. "So what is your plan, Jake?"

"I step into Max's life. I'm confident no one will know the difference."

"How will you explain having been gone for so long?"

"I was in a car accident." He held up his arm, which held a cast from hand to elbow. "I have the broken bone to prove it. Plus, Max's boss had his medical records sealed then created fake ones to show he was in a coma but ultimately came through it. He also adjusted the official police report of the crash to remove any mention of me or that Max was killed. Anyone who checks it out will find out just what we want them to know—that Max was injured in a car wreck and was hospitalized for three weeks before being released. If there's something I don't know or can't figure out, I figure I'll blame it on memory loss from the accident."

She nodded in a gesture he hoped meant she thought it was a decent plan. It wasn't perfect but it was all he had and he really believed he could make it work.

She glanced at her watch then stood.

"I should go. I need to prep for an early morning surprise visit to Dale Lowrey's apartment with his parole officer. I feel certain we'll find some drugs and that will give me a reason to bring him in and question him about Creed."

The name sounded familiar but Jake couldn't place it. "Is that one of Creed's crew?"

She shot him a concerned look. "Yes. Dale's been working for Creed practically since middle school. He's been busted multiple times for selling drugs downtown and just got out of prison early for good behavior on a four-year stint for robbery six months ago. I've been keeping a close eye on him. I'm hoping I can convince him to turn on Creed. If he doesn't, he'll have to go back to jail and finish out his time for breaking his parole if we find drugs in his place."

He stopped himself before he warned her to be careful dealing with Lowrey. She was a trained deputy and didn't need him second-guessing her. Yet he was surprised at how easily the worry came to him where she was concerned.

"I hope you find the evidence you need."

"Thank you. I'm sure he's moving drugs for Creed again. Hopefully, an early morning raid will find it. My mom will be out of town so I'll have to find someone to take Robby to school but I'll work it out."

"Robby?" That had been her brother's name but he was dead so she couldn't be referring to him.

She stopped herself and her eyes widened. She gulped. "My son. He's four years old."

That news hit him like a ton of bricks. Sabrina was a mom. He took a moment to catch his breath before responding. "I'm sorry. I didn't know. Max never mentioned it. I didn't even know you'd gotten married." He'd thought he'd prepared himself for every sting but that was one he hadn't anticipated.

"I'm not married. Robby's father..."
Confusion clouded her face and she
seemed to struggle for words then finally
gave a loud sigh. "It's too complicated
to go into right now. I really should go.
Give me your phone."

He pulled his cell from his pocket and
handed it to her. "Why?"

She quickly entered a phone number
and contact information into it. "Max
and I used the code name Tiffany Matthews in case anyone looked through his
contact list. The cover was that she's an
old girlfriend that he still occasionally
saw. I even have a social media account
set up for her in case anyone goes looking. If you need to reach me, call me at
that number." He took his phone back
as she grabbed her purse and walked to
the door. She stopped and turned to him.
"Stay safe, Jake."

He nodded and repeated the phrase
back to her. "Stay safe, Sabrina."

He waited until after she'd disappeared

up the hallway then slipped out the back entrance and to his car. He hadn't come to town to reconnect with Sabrina Reagan but it had been good to see her again and know that she was doing better. Why hadn't his brother mentioned they were working together? He grimaced. He knew why. Max understood how difficult it had been for Jake to walk away from the only woman he'd ever loved.

And all those old protective feelings about her had resurfaced once he was around her. Only she wasn't that same devastated woman he'd left behind. She'd pulled herself together, started a career and a family, and looked to be strong and determined in her mission. But he'd seen a hint of the kind person he'd once known when she'd worried about his safety and the funny Sabrina in her Tiffany Matthews cover. That had been the name that had once adorned her fake ID in high school and he imagined Tiffany's social media page would have old photos of her and Jake together.

He shook off those nostalgic memories. He couldn't allow Sabrina's presence to affect his mission. He was in town to bring down a drug dealer, not rekindle a long-ago romance.

TWO

Max's cell phone had been damaged in the accident so Jake had cloned it. He had multiple messages from a cell phone number that he didn't recognize but assumed it was Creed's number based on the messages.

Where are you?

Why haven't you responded?

You'd better be dead.

That last one had hurt when Jake had read it.

Now that he was back in town, he

needed to make contact and reestablish Max as a member of Creed's team.

He'd stopped by the sheriff's office first after arriving in Mercy County. Now he turned his rental car toward the small apartment complex where his brother had leased an apartment. He parked then grabbed his bag and walked up to Max's door. He unlocked it then walked inside and shed his bag and jacket, momentarily overwhelmed by his brother's presence. This might have been his undercover home but it still had his feeling to it. Although there were no photographs of family or friends, necessary to keep them safe, the big-screen TV, oversize couch and sports memorabilia decorated the room. A circular table and chairs sat to the side near the small kitchen. The coffeemaker on the counter appeared to be the most used appliance given the multiple mugs sitting beside it. Jake opened the refrigerator. It was empty except for a twelve-pack case of soda with a few cans missing. Apparently, his brother had eaten out a lot based on the lack of groceries in his apartment.

A swell of grief pulsed through him. Jake slammed shut the refrigerator and shoved those emotions as far back as he could. He'd been fighting them ever since he'd decided to take on this mission. He couldn't grieve his brother and be his brother at the same time.

A knock on the door grabbed his attention. He tensed and reached for the gun in the holster at his side. He glanced through the peephole and saw two men standing outside. He spotted guns beneath their jackets. Creed's men. Had to be.

He slipped the gun back into its holster. This was the risk he'd agreed to take upon assuming his brother's identity. Max would know these guys.

He opened the door and tried his best

to look unflustered. He nodded at them. "How's it going, fellas?"

He didn't recognize either man from their photos but that didn't mean anything. He knew the lower men in the organization came and went. Sabrina might recognize them. He should have asked her about those members she was targeting.

The bigger of the two did the speaking. "Creed wants to see you."

Jake leaned against the door. "How did he know I was back?"

"He's had someone watching your apartment. Wanted us to bring you in if you showed your face here again. We were driving by and saw the lights on."

He nodded and took a deep breath. *Here we go.* "Let me get my coat." He left the door open as he reached for his jacket and slid it on. These men hadn't blinked at seeing him so they believed he was Max, only he had no idea how well they'd known his brother. They weren't the ones he needed to be concerned about.

He followed them downstairs then slid into the back seat of their car and watched as they headed to the edge of town toward the old industrial area then stopped in front of an old abandoned warehouse. A tall chain-link fence with a privacy liner hid the building but it was opened from inside so they could drive through. On the other side of the fence, he spotted cars in all forms of disrepair. Obviously a chop shop. It seemed drugs weren't Creed's only business. Once they arrived, the two men escorted Jake through the building and up a set of stairs to an office on a second floor.

He tensed as they opened the door and, for the first time, had second thoughts about this. Too late now. He was here and was about to find out if his ruse could fool anyone. He steadied his breath, then stepped into the room. A man stood at the window and turned to him. Jake recognized him from his photographs. Paul Creed. The leader of this drug ring and the man his brother had fought to bring to justice.

Jake's pulse kicked up a notch and he felt sweat beading on his forehead as Creed stared at him. This was the moment of truth. Was he going to have to fight his way out of here? His hand itched to reach for his gun but he resisted. He couldn't make the first move and jeopardize his undercover identity.

Finally, Creed spoke. "Take a seat," he said, motioning to a chair sitting in front of a desk.

Jake pulled it up and sat down.

"We've all been wondering where you've been." He motioned to the cast on Jake's arm. "Looks like you've had some trouble the last few weeks."

Jake held up his arm then nodded. "You could say that. I was in a car accident. My car slid off the road and rammed a tree. I woke in the hospital bed and learned I'd been in a medically induced coma for several weeks to treat some brain swelling. Ultimately, I made it out alive with a concussion, a broken wrist and some cuts and bruises."

"How terrible. I wish you'd let someone know. I would have sent flowers."

"I appreciate that but, like I said, I was out of it for several weeks and once I did wake up, my phone was smashed in the wreck. I lost all of my numbers so I had no way to contact anyone. I headed back to town as soon as I was able."

Creed stood then slid into the big chair behind the desk. The shape of his shoulders was less tense, which implied that he believed Jake's story. He started to relax a bit himself.

"For a while there we were wondering if you'd skipped town. Some of the men even wondered if perhaps you vanished so suddenly because you were a cop." Max had mentioned one of Creed's lieutenants—Jacoby—didn't trust him and looked for any opportunity to undermine him to Creed.

He shook his head. "It wasn't my intention to be gone so long. I'd planned to spend the weekend with a lady friend of mine out of town but I never made it. If you're still not convinced, I'd be happy to email you a copy of the accident report or my hospital bill as proof."

Creed chuckled and Jake knew he believed the story. "I'm glad you're better, my friend. I would appreciate if you could send me a copy of that accident report though."

That request didn't bother Jake since he was sure Creed was only being thorough. He could see by the way he'd relaxed that he'd bought every word and didn't doubt Jake was who he said he was and what had happened. He'd believed that no one would be able to tell him from Max and it seemed he was right. And, if anyone noticed any differences, he could also use the excuse of the wreck and head trauma to explain it away.

"I'll have Joe and Tony drive you back to your apartment to rest for the night then we'll start back to work bright and early tomorrow."

"I've had weeks of rest. I'm ready to start now. Before I left, we were preparing for a big shipment coming in about a month. Did I miss that?"

"No, we had to push taking control of the product back a few weeks thanks to some local law-enforcement issues. The sheriff's office staked out the river dock where we were supposed to make the trade-off."

"How did they know you were doing it there?"

"We don't know. That's when some people began to suspect you, Max."

Had his brother known the location and passed it on to Sabrina? He didn't know and he wasn't going to risk giving away that he didn't know either unless he was forced to. "Obviously, it wasn't me. I planned on being here for it. Now I can be. What can I do to help?"

"I've got Jacoby already procuring trucks. I was able to put off my supplier for a few weeks but he won't be happy if we have another issue. And these aren't the type of men you want to make angry. Our biggest problem is a local Mercy County deputy who has been targeting my men. Deputy Reagan. She's been a complication."

Jake was surprised he knew Sabrina by name. A part of him was proud that she'd made such a headache for Creed and his men. The other side of him was horrified that she'd made herself such a target.

She'd always been stubborn and determined. It had been one of the things he'd most admired about her and that was before she'd made it her job to bring down Creed. Her brother's death had sent her on a mission.

He had to remind himself that she was a well-trained officer of the law and it wasn't fair of him to keep thinking of her as someone in need of rescue. She was determined to get Creed and it wasn't right of him to try to stop her.

Besides, he was glad to have someone on his side who knew the truth about him. Hiding his identity wasn't that big of a deal for him. He'd worked under-cover multiple times before. But having someone he didn't have to hide from was comforting.

Creed's cell phone rang and he pulled it from his pocket then glanced at the screen. "I need to deal with this."

Creed stood and walked out as he answered the call. He left Jake alone in the office. Did he normally do that? It felt like a trap that Jake could easily walk into. However, he couldn't allow this opportunity to pass.

Either this was a test of his loyalty or Creed trusted Max completely.

He prayed it was the second one.

Once Creed was out of the room, Jake made his way around the desk and tapped on his computer. If the names of his suppliers were in there, he needed to find them. Maybe he could end this charade before it really got started.

He pulled a flash drive from his pocket, slid it into the drive on Creed's computer then started the process of copying it. It would be easier to search through once he was somewhere safe and alone. He watched the door, praying that Creed didn't return before the copy was done.

He heard Creed's voice as he headed back so Jake pulled the flash drive from the laptop and closed it.

Creed entered the room and motioned to Jake to follow him. He led the way back down the staircase and toward a waiting car. "I'm glad to have you back, Max." He opened the back car door. "But I've got meetings tonight that were already scheduled. I'll meet you back here in the morning and we'll discuss our next steps in getting our shipments ready."

Max climbed back into the back of the car and Creed closed the door.

He fingered the flash drive in his pocket and hoped that Creed hadn't had cameras set up in the room. He didn't breathe easy again until the car pulled into his apartment complex parking lot and stopped close to his building.

"Do we need to pick you up tomorrow?" Tony, the driver, asked.

He shook his head. "No. I have a rental car."

He got out and slammed the door then walked up to his apartment. Once he was alone and the door was locked, he pulled out the flash drive. This might be all the ammunition he needed to bring down Creed and his supplier. He dug his laptop from his bag then inserted the flash drive. The screen filled with a bunch of indecipherable gibberish.

Encrypted.

He rubbed his face. Of course it wouldn't be that easy.

He pulled out his cell phone and called Sabrina's number. She didn't answer so he left a voicemail, hoping she checked her messages soon. "We need to meet," he told her.

He wasn't entirely sure that he'd read Creed right. It had seemed too easy to step into Max's role and his instincts were on high alert. Either Max had been really good at gaining Creed's trust or else Creed was giving him a long leash to strangle himself with.

He ordered take-out then settled in front of the TV and did his best to drown out the silence of the empty apartment. He didn't like it. It gave him too much time to think about his brother and how he would never see him again. They hadn't been good at staying in touch throughout the years since they'd both chosen to focus on their respective careers, Max's with the DEA and Jake's as a detective with the San Antonio PD.

Finally, he couldn't take the silence any longer. He grabbed his keys and headed toward the sheriff's office, hoping that Sabrina had gotten his message. He took the long way, driving at times fast and erratic and at other times slow and cautiously, making certain that no one was following behind him.

He pulled into the back parking lot and parked. However, before he got out, he spotted another car across the street. It was sitting with its lights off and someone crouched behind the steering wheel.

He closed the door and watched it. Something about the car seemed out of place and it raised the hairs on the back of his neck.

The back door to the sheriff's office opened and Sabrina exited and walked to her car. He watched her as she climbed in, started the engine and pulled away. As she turned out of the parking lot, the mysterious car started its engine and followed her.

Jake's gut clenched. He'd been right about that car. He started his rental then pulled out behind the trailing car. Like the car he was following, he kept his lights off and operated under the cover of dark. He had a bad feeling about this. Was this what Creed had meant when he'd talked about taking care of the problem?

He hit the redial button on his cell phone and hoped Sabrina answered this time.

She did after several rings. "Hello?"

"Sabrina, it's Jake. I'm behind you but there's another car following you too."

"I don't see it."

"It's driving without lights and keeping its distance but I'm sure he's following you. I watched him as he got behind you when you left the parking lot. It's possible he's trying to follow you to your home to figure out where you live or he might be waiting for a moment to run you off the road."

"I don't care for either of those scenarios."

"I'll keep following him but I wouldn't recommend going home."

"Don't worry. I won't. I'm calling for backup. But you need to be careful too, Jake. You don't want to be seen helping me."

If it came down to it, he knew he would choose to help her and burn his undercover mission but he didn't think that would happen. He was in a nondescript rental car and no one in Creed's organization had seen him driving it. Plus, thanks to daylight savings time and few roadside lights, it was already pitch-dark out. He would act if he had to and hope the darkness covered his identity but that was a last resort.

He listened as she used the radio to call for assistance. He recognized the road they were on. A mile or so up the road, it became more barren with fewer lights and businesses. At least, it used to be that way when he was growing up here. If he was right, that was where this car and its sketchy occupant would make its move.

He was right. They made the curve and suddenly the car turned its lights on and sped up, pulling up beside Sabrina's vehicle. Jake sped up too. He had to do his best to keep this driver from running her off the road while also maintaining his cover.

Sabrina sped up too but the sedan kept up with her and tried to force her off the road. Jake didn't know what his plan was. If he wanted her to wreck or pull over so he could abduct her. Either way, he couldn't allow it.

He was just about to hit the gas and slide into the other lane to engage with the car when sirens and flashing lights overtook him as two patrol cars roared up behind him. They came alongside the car and forced them to pull over to the shoulder.

Jake slowed down then moved to the other lane and passed them, noting not only a driver but a passenger he hadn't noticed earlier. He breathed a sigh of relief that the deputies would handle the situation and detain them at least long enough for Sabrina to get home safely.

A mile or so up the road as the streetlights resumed, Sabrina's vehicle pulled to the shoulder and stopped. Jake did the same then hopped out and hurried to check on her. She let the window down and he leaned in. Her hands were clenched on the steering wheel and she looked shaken but at least she was alive.

"Are you okay?"

She nodded but kept her hands clenched on the steering wheel. "That was too close."

"You shouldn't go home. They might try to find you at your house."

She nodded again. "I'll go to my mom's place. She has Robby there."

"I'll follow behind you to make sure you make it there safely and aren't followed."

He thought for a moment that she might protest that and insist that she didn't need his help but she finally gave him a nod. "Okay. Thank you. If you hadn't been here, I don't know what would have happened."

"You would have handled it on your own, but I'm glad I was there and saw them."

"Why were you at the sheriff's office?"

He reached into his pocket and pulled out the flash drive. "I took this from Creed's laptop but it's encrypted. I was hoping someone from your office could break it."

She nodded then took it from him. "I'll give it to Jana Carter tomorrow. She's our IT guru."

He climbed back into his car after giving the area a quick scan. The road here was flat and he could see in several directions pretty far. No one was around to follow them. He was going to make sure she made it safely home but he also didn't want his cover blown.

He followed behind as she drove to a subdivision on the outskirts of town. The last time he'd seen her, her family had lived closer to town but things had obviously changed. Her mother had moved and Sabrina now had a son.

He drew a deep breath as that last one affected him again. So many changes.

She pulled into a driveway and he parked on the curb and got out. "Nice place," he told her.

"My mom moved here after my dad died last year. Few people know it so it's a safe place for her and Robby."

Robby. Her son. "You named him after your brother. That's nice."

She nodded. "Having him was the only thing that kept me going. I knew I had to figure out a way to keep living for my son's sake."

He was glad she'd found a reason. When he'd left her, she'd been in a very dark place that he hadn't been able to reach. She'd needed a reason to live and it hadn't been him or the future he'd wanted for them together.

But knowing that she'd found someone else, someone who could reach her, who could give her a reason to go on, bothered him at a level he didn't want to admit. He didn't like that someone else had been able to give her what he couldn't.

Only, she hadn't mentioned a husband. Complicated is what she'd called it. Divorce? Widowed? She still had the same name. Perhaps Robby's father had been nothing more than a moment of passion. He didn't care for any of those options.

He paused and did the math. Robby was four years old. Five years since he'd left her. Could it be…?

He dismissed that notion. She would never have kept something like that from him.

Sabrina walked to the front door and produced a key and unlocked the door. She stepped inside. The house seemed quiet but he spotted the light from a television off to the right in what appeared to be the living room.

"Mom?"

A woman poked her head from the kitchen. He recognized her as Beverly Reagan, Sabrina's mother. She was a few years older and grayer but hadn't changed much as far as he could tell. "In the kitchen," she called out.

They stepped into the living room and he spotted a child curled up on the sofa. He was cute with dark hair and dimples, features he definitely thought he recognized. Sabrina reached down and pulled him to her, taking him into her arms. He gave her a hug then locked blue eyes with

Jake, eyes so much like his and Max's that it caught his breath.

"Who's he, Momma?" the boy asked in a sweet high-pitched voice.

Sabrina glanced back at Jake then placed him back down. "This is my friend. Go in the bedroom and play, Robby. We'll be going home in a bit."

The little boy hurried to do as he was told.

Sabrina opened her mouth to say something but her mother chose that moment to walk in from the kitchen. "Max, it's good to see you again."

Sabrina looked like she started to correct her mother then changed her mind. She pulled out her cell phone then plugged it into the charger on the counter. She was avoiding his eyes and the conversation they were going to have to have.

He took the hint and extended his hand. "It's good to see you again too, Beverly." He wondered if Max had spent time with Sabrina and her family enough for her mother to remember him from when they were kids. That wasn't his business. He and Sabrina had had a professional relationship but they had once all been friends when the three of them attended school together.

"Coffee?" Mrs. Reagan asked.

"It's late, Mom. I don't think Max wants—"

"I'd love some," he interrupted. "I probably won't sleep anyway but coffee doesn't really keep me up." He suddenly had something that would definitely prevent him from sleeping.

Mrs. Reagan stepped back into the kitchen, poured coffee into a mug then handed it to him. He sipped it. "It's good. Thank you."

"I'm glad you finally made it back to town. My daughter has been very worried about you. You shouldn't have stayed away so long without letting her know. I'd begun to wonder if you'd left her the same way that no-good brother of yours did."

Sabrina's eyes widened and she shot him an *I'm sorry* look. It wasn't necessary. He wasn't proud of the way he'd left her and they hadn't really discussed it.

He held up his hand to assure her he wasn't going to reveal himself to her mother. "I shouldn't have stayed away for so long. I've already given my explanation and apologies to Sabrina."

"It's okay, Mom. Max didn't abandon us. He was in a car accident." She motioned toward the cast on his arm. "He's back now and we're still working on bringing down Paul Creed."

Beverly waved her hand at Sabrina to stop. "I don't like to hear about what you're doing, Sabrina, but I'm glad you have Max to watch out for you. Besides, Robby's been asking about his uncle Max."

Sabrina spit out her coffee. "Mom!" Her face reddened.

Uncle Max. Confirmation for what he already suspected.

He looked at Sabrina, who was staring past him. He turned. Her little boy stood in the doorway of the kitchen clutching a stuffed animal. "I'm ready to go home, Momma."

Sabrina rushed to him and scooped him up into her arms. "Honey, we're going home in a bit." She headed down the hall to the playroom.

Jake dropped his coffee mug onto the table then walked back into the living room. Photographs of Sabrina and the boy were shown prominently. He saw the resemblance clearly now. The same nose. Blue eyes and dark hair he and his brother shared. No denying it.

And Max had known. They'd spent hours together and his brother hadn't mentioned Sabrina had had his child.

Why didn't you tell me, Max?

"Jake."

He turned. Sabrina stood in the hallway entrance. He couldn't look at her knowing what she'd kept from him.

"Let me explain."

He put up his hand to stop her. "I don't want to hear it." He beelined for the door. Suddenly, the air was sparse and he needed to get out of there before more truths tumbled on him.

He'd already lost so much that he was struggling to keep control of his emotions. He couldn't handle this on top of it.

He forwent the sidewalk and stepped through the grass to get to his car parked at the curb. Sabrina was right behind him.

She grabbed his arm in an attempt to stop him. "Jake, please. Let me explain."

He couldn't hold it back any longer. He jerked his arm away and spun on her. "Explain what? That you lied to me? That you kept something this important from me?"

She lowered her head. "I'm sorry."

"Did Max know?" She hesitated to answer. "Did he?"

Finally, she nodded. "Yes, he knew. He figured it out. He wanted to tell you but I begged him to let me be the one."

"But you didn't."

"I didn't know how to tell you." A tear slipped down her face. He checked the urge to wipe it away and comfort her. That was messed up. He was the wronged one, not her.

"You know how bad it was for me when my brother died. I was distraught. I didn't want to go on. I didn't know how to move forward. You had already left town when I discovered I was pregnant. Knowing that I had this child growing inside me was the only thing that kept me going. Robby brought me back to life."

"You still kept it from me. I had a right to know I had a son."

"I could barely function for myself and Robby, much less think about you. I was suddenly a single mom with a baby. I was overwhelmed and scared out of my mind. I know I should have told you but I was fighting so hard to get back to a normal, stable life."

His anger turned to agony that he hadn't been there for her. "I would have helped you, Sabrina. I would have done anything to help you."

"I know." Now the tears did flow. "I wasn't in a place to want your help. I'm sorry for how I treated you, Jake, and I'm sorry for keeping this from you. I did try to reach out to you a couple of years ago. I wrote you a letter telling you all about Robby, but I never heard back from you so I assumed you got it and decided you didn't want to be a part of his life."

"I never received any letter."

"I realize that now. The last I'd heard, when you left town, you were joining the Dallas police department. That's where I sent it."

He'd left Dallas soon after his arrival

and gone to San Antonio. And his undercover work had caused him to avoid social media or anything that might give up his identity. That could explain why she hadn't been able to locate him.

"When Max showed up in town and found out about Robby, he insisted there was no way you received that letter and decided not to see Robby. That's when I realized you must not have gotten it. He told me then where you were and said to contact you again. He said if I didn't, he would. I was working up my nerve when he suddenly vanished."

That stung to know that his brother had kept this from him. He should have come out and told him the truth despite Sabrina's request. He'd had a right to know.

He pulled open the car door. "I have to go."

"Jake." He stopped and looked back at her. "I truly am sorry."

He climbed into the car and started the engine. He couldn't look at her. She'd kept something so big and fundamental from him.

As he drove away, he couldn't turn his mind from the little boy with the wide grin and blue eyes.

He was a father.

THREE

Well, that had not gone the way she'd hoped.

Sabrina wiped the tears from her face as she watched the car disappear around the corner. The pain and anger in Jake's face, the look of betrayal, had rocked her. She'd never meant for any of this to happen.

She marched back into the house and confronted her mother. "Why would you say that?"

Her mother's eyes widened in an innocent expression. "What did I say? Max knows about Robby. We spoke about it the last time he was here. He loves that little boy."

"No, Mother, you don't understand.

That wasn't Max. That was Jake pretending to be Max."

Her mom's brows crunched. "Why would he pretend to be his brother?"

"Because Max was killed in a car wreck a few weeks ago. He was working undercover in Paul Creed's organization. Jake came to town to finish that but he has to pretend to be Max in order to do it." She sighed. "I shouldn't have even told you that. It could compromise his cover."

Realization dawned on her mom's face and she slid into a chair. "You mean, I just told Jake Harris that he's Robby's father? Oh, honey, I'm sorry. I didn't mean—"

Sabrina fell into a chair, defeated. "No, it's not your fault, Mom. I should have told him a long time ago, then this wouldn't have happened. I should have been honest with him. Besides, I'm pretty sure he'd figured it out before your slip-up."

"After the way he left you, I can understand your not wanting to share Robby with him."

"I've been angry at Jake for a long time but the truth is that I pushed him away, Mom. You know how I was. I was inconsolable after Robby's death. I don't blame Jake for leaving. There was nothing he could do for me. I wish I'd responded better but I didn't."

"You can't blame someone for how they grieve."

"I know but I was just so angry. I didn't even want Jake around me. I didn't want to continue living. Now I know how my actions then hurt everyone. I robbed Jake of being a father and I robbed my son of having a father. I tried to apologize to him but he wouldn't listen to me."

Her mom reached her hand across the table and placed her hand over Sabrina's. "Give him some time, honey. He'll come around."

She was grateful for her mother's support and prayed she was right. She couldn't really blame her. Sabrina was the one who'd kept the truth from Jake. She was the one to blame for his anger.

She quickly changed the subject to something more pleasing. "Have you packed for your weekend getaway with Bob?"

Her mom's face brightened at the mention of her trip. "I haven't even started packing. I can't decide what to bring and, you know me, I'd pack my entire closet if I could."

Sabrina stood and motioned to her. "Come on. I'll help you choose a few outfits before I leave."

They spent the next hour rummaging through the closet picking out things to pack until her mom's suitcase was ready to go. Her mother gushed with the heady excitement of new love. Sabrina was happy for her but realized she'd hadn't felt that feeling in a long time. Not since her early days with Jake. Back when her brother and father were alive and anything in life seemed possible.

She glanced at the clock. It was late and she still had that early shift. "We should head home." She pulled her mom into a hug. "Have a fun trip and tell Bob I said hello."

She walked down the hall to the second bedroom that had been designated as a playroom and where Robby slept whenever he stayed over. She opened the door and peered inside. He'd fallen asleep on the floor. She wasn't surprised given the lateness of the hour. She pushed his hair back and gave him a kiss on the forehead before carrying him out to the SUV and loading him into the car seat. He didn't even rouse as she buckled him up. She'd never known such love as she had for this little boy. She hadn't believed it was possible to feel anything again after her brother died but little Robby had opened up her heart and helped her heal from her pain. It had been a long hard road, but she'd finally come out on the other side.

She owed Jake the truth. He hadn't deserved to find out he was a father that way. Max had been right to press her to contact him and now she wished she'd had the courage to do so earlier.

She hoped Jake could forgive her. Her mother was right. Robby needed his father. She prayed he wouldn't hold her sins against their child.

Jake had been driving aimlessly, trying to figure a way to wrap his brain around this new knowledge. He was a father. Had been a father for years and Sabrina hadn't told him.

He gripped the steering wheel tighter as worry wove its way through him. He didn't have a great role model when it came to fathers. His and Max's was a major alcoholic who'd finally drunk himself to death a few years after he and his brother had left town. They'd returned briefly to close up the house and scatter their dad's ashes.

Sabrina had been his rock during that

difficult time. He'd done his best to keep his emotions in check. He and Max had both suffered at their father's hands and his feelings about his dad were convoluted but he had been their father. Sabrina had seen past Jake's flippant attitude to the real grief. She'd been there for him but he hadn't done the same for her when it mattered the most.

Now she'd lied to him in the worst possible way.

He turned the car toward the industrial side of town back toward the factory Creed worked out of. He needed to get back into his undercover persona and the mission. He would think about Sabrina and Robby once this was all said and done.

The parking lot was crowded and when he entered, so was the factory floor which surprised him. A crowd of men were standing around in a circle and someone from the center was speaking.

Jake couldn't see the man or hear his words over the rumble of the group.

Suddenly, the crowd broke up and Paul Creed stepped out. He spotted Jake and looked surprised. "You're back."

"Yeah, I am. What's going on here?" These men hadn't been here when he'd left.

Creed motioned him to follow him up to his office.

Once they were inside, Jake looked at him. "What's up? It's kinda late to have a meeting, isn't it?"

"It's not actually. I've got men about to bring product into several nightclubs in the area. They're picking up. The real parties don't get started until close to midnight."

Jake nodded then mentally kicked himself for that slip-up. Max would have known that. Had he blown it?

"Since you're here, you should know I got word from my supplier earlier tonight. They're unhappy with the fact that

Deputy Reagan keeps interfering. They want her taken care of as soon as possible."

He felt his jaw clench. He was targeting Sabrina? "I think you mentioned that earlier."

"I'm officially placing a hit on the deputy. She won't be bothering us anymore. I just told several of my men to take care of her tonight."

For once, he was glad he'd trained himself to keep his emotions in check. He wanted to scream and take this man down until he rescinded that hit. But he had to think about getting to Sabrina first.

"Are they going to hit her at her house?"

He nodded. "They're heading there now. And I've given them instructions not to leave any witnesses."

His hands began to sweat. He needed a reason to get out of here and warn her about the impending strike. They knew where she was and they were coming after her and Robby.

They were targeting his family.

"Why don't you call it off and let me see to it?" he suggested. That would the easiest thing for him. Convince Creed to call off the hit and let him take care of her.

"No, I have another assignment for you, Max. I'll fill you in tomorrow. I'm still making plans."

"I can help with those plans, Paul."

Creed looked at Jake for a split second too long in his opinion before refusing his help. "I'll let you know when I need you."

Jake could see it in his face. He didn't trust him completely. Whatever trust Max had built with him had evaporated during the time he'd been away. He was still questioning him. Or maybe it was because he somehow sensed that Jake wasn't Max.

He could wonder about that later. For

now, he needed to warn Sabrina that her life was in danger.

He waited until he was on the road to call her cell phone. It rang and rang and then clicked over to voicemail. He left a message to call him back and that Creed had placed a price on her head.

He tried her cell phone again and then again and was about to give up and call into the sheriff's office when someone answered.

"Hello?"

"Sabrina, it's Jake. Finally."

"This isn't Sabrina. It's her mother. Jake, I'm so—"

"No time for apologies, Bev. I need to talk to Sabrina."

"She's not here. She and Robby went home. I guess she forgot she'd put her phone on the charger here in my kitchen because she left it."

So he had no way to contact her. "Does she have another cell phone or a landline at her house? Any other way I can get in touch with her?"

"No. I was going to leave it. I figured she would come by and get it tomorrow morning. I'm getting ready to leave on a trip or else I would take it to her. Is everything okay?"

"Definitely not. I need her address now. Where does she live?"

She must have heard the urgency in his voice because she rattled off the address and he quickly keyed it into his GPS.

"She's in danger, isn't she?"

"Yes, she is but I'm on my way to her and Robby."

"What can I do?"

"Call the sheriff's office and tell them she's in trouble. They need to send a team to her house."

"Okay, I will. Take care of them, Jake."

"I will." He ended the call. He'd already turned the car toward the directions the GPS indicated. He knew that part of town and it would take him fifteen minutes to get there. He had no idea where Creed's men were or when they'd left.

He didn't breathe until he turned on her street. As he neared her house, he scoured the street for something or someone out of place. He found it. A car several houses down with four men inside. They were watching the house on the corner. The house's Christmas lights were lit up and the tree in the window shone. Sabrina was standing in the driveway next to her car getting Robby out of his car seat.

Jake pulled to the curb behind another parked vehicle and cut the engine. He saw activity in the car and knew they were getting ready to strike. If he had to burn his cover, he would do so, but he hoped it wouldn't come to that. He slipped a baseball cap over his head then got out and darted across the neighbor's lawn in the dark of night toward her house. As he reached her driveway, he heard the car down the street rev its engine.

They were coming.

Sabrina spotted him as she pulled Robby from the car and into her arms. "Jake, what on earth?"

"Get inside the house now." He pressed them and she ran without question toward the front door. She quickly unlocked it and hurried inside. He shut the door.

"What's happening?"

"Men with guns." He reached for his own weapon, then peeked out the front window and saw the car speed up to the front of the house then squeal to a stop. Two men with guns leaned out and started firing.

"Get down!" he shouted as the clatter of gunfire hit the house and burst through the walls and windows. Robby screamed and started crying as Sabrina covered him with her body. The Christmas tree hit the floor and she darted into the kitchen carrying Robby in her arms.

Jake scrambled to follow them as another round of bullets kept coming. He pressed them both toward the back of the house and crouched behind the kitchen island. Jake still had a clear view of the front window. The car was still there and the men were now getting out and approaching the house.

Robby cried and Sabrina did her best to comfort him and keep him quiet.

"Why is this happening?" she demanded.

"Creed put a hit out on you. His suppliers want you out of the picture."

She clutched Robby and he could see that news shook her. It had shaken him too. But now, more than her life was at risk.

She reached into her pocket then her face fell even further. "I don't have my phone to call for help. You?"

He'd left his in the car in the rush to get out. "It's been done. Your mom is calling in the cavalry." He saw her surprise. "You left your phone at her house. She's the one who told me where you lived."

She rubbed Robby's hair and did her best to soothe him but he could see fear in her face.

"What are they doing?"

"Getting out of the car. They're approaching the house. Do you have a safe room or any other way out of the house?"

She shook her head. "The backyard is gated. We'd have to climb over it and my neighbor has a big, mean dog."

So they were trapped.

He heard boots on the driveway and knew they were close. Armed men were about to break down the front door and kill his child and the woman he'd once wanted to marry and build a life with. And he wouldn't be spared either. Creed had ordered no witnesses. That included him.

He rubbed the back of his neck as the truth settled in.

They were in trouble.

Sabrina pushed over the kitchen table then settled Robby behind it. He was whimpering but had stopped wailing. She grabbed her weapon then took up a spot beside him. "We only need to hold on until my department arrives."

He admired her bravado and wished he had more time to observe it. She wasn't going down without a fight.

Sirens in the distance were a welcome sound. The gunmen heard them approaching and ran back to their vehicle. They sped off as the first cruisers from the sheriff's office surrounded the house.

A wave of gratitude washed through him. *Thank You, God.* "The cavalry is here," he told her.

Sabrina put away her weapon then retrieved Robby from behind the table and rocked him on her hip. "It's okay, baby. We're okay now." She rubbed the back of his head then looked at Jake. "Let me go out first. We don't want anyone mistaking you for one of the shooters."

He agreed and let them go first. Not everyone in the sheriff's office knew who he was. In fact, most people didn't. That was the point. That everyone thought he was one of Creed's men. Only he didn't need that trouble today.

Kent hurried over to them and touched her arm. "Are you okay?"

She nodded but continued to clutch Robby. "Yes, we're fine thanks to him."

Kent shook Jake's hand. "Glad to have you back, Max. Thank you for looking out for them. Now, does someone want to tell me what happened?"

They waited until a paramedic had Robby in the back of an ambulance checking him over before he and Sabrina addressed Kent. "Creed told me that his suppliers wanted Sabrina dead. I tried to call her to warn her but she'd left her phone at her mother's. When I arrived, I spotted the car down the road loaded with men and guns. I knew I had to get them to safety."

She touched his arm, sending a spark through him. "You saved our lives," she said, glancing up at him with appreciation in her gaze. "I can't thank you enough."

The anger he'd felt for her earlier that evening had faded in the wake of her and Robby nearly being killed. "You can thank me by backing off of this investigation into Creed."

She pulled her hand away as if he'd pinched her. "You know I can't do that."

Irritation flooded him. She had a child to think about. It wasn't right that she was placing him in danger too with her recklessness. "Sabrina, you have to think about your safety. Creed has put a price on your head. Every lowlife thug in his crew will be gunning for you. It isn't only your life you're placing in danger. It's Robby's too. No witnesses. That was his order."

That point seemed to reach her. She

bit her lower lip the way he'd seen her do when she was trying to think things through. "You're right. I can't put Robby's life in danger that way."

He breathed a sigh of relief. "Good. Then you'll back off the investigation?"

"No. But I will leave Robby with my mom. I hate to ask her to cancel her plans but she will for this. The house is still technically listed under the previous owner's name and few people know she's moved. He'll be safe there."

"I have to agree with Max," Kent interjected. "You have no idea who could be after you now."

"That's always been true, hasn't it? I've already been targeted twice before the hit. I'll stay close to the station but I'm not backing down. I won't let Paul Creed send me into hiding."

Jake shared a concerned look with Kent but he gave in to her. "Okay, but you'll be careful and you won't make a move without letting me know," Kent in-

structed her. "You're never to go anywhere alone either. You need backup."

Jake could see she didn't like that one
detail but she nodded. "Fine. I won't go
anywhere alone."

"Good. I'll also double patrols on your
mom's neighborhood to keep an eye out
for suspicious behavior. In the meantime,
we've got a team canvassing this neighborhood for witnesses or video of the car
and the men. I've also got roadblocks set
up. We'll find the men who did this."

What they would find were dangerous men to be sure, but men looking to
score a hefty payday. Jake hoped they
would roll over on Creed for giving the
kill order but first they had to capture
them.

He glanced around at all the deputies
and crime scene techs on the scene. In
addition, a crowd of nosy neighbors had
circled around the lawn despite the late
hour. And once the TV news crews arrived, all this might be on television.

He was exposed out here. His identity in danger. He didn't know if the men who'd shot at the house had recognized him or not but he needed to keep his undercover identity in check in case he hadn't been compromised.

"I need to get out of here," he whispered to Sabrina.

She nodded then looked toward the ambulance where Robby was clutching his toy bear. He'd finally stopped crying but hadn't settled completely from all the chaos of what had just happened. "I should get him to my mother's." She glanced at her car. It was littered with bullet holes as was the house. Glass scattered on the ground and her Christmas tree was protruding through the front window.

His car parked down the street was still drivable. "I'll take you both over there."

But they needed to go before more people arrived who might decide to follow them. Since the moment he'd seen her again, his protective instincts had kicked in. And learning that he had a son had only intensified that desire. He might be angry with her and confused about his feelings about Robby but one emotion was pushing its way to the forefront of his consciousness.

He would do whatever it took to keep his family safe.

FOUR

Sabrina's heart finally stopped racing with fear and adrenaline as Jake turned onto her mother's street. Cold anger replaced it. Anger that Creed had sent men to her house. Around her son. She clutched Robby as Jake drove. She didn't even have a car seat so Jake was being extra careful while also watching his rearview mirror and checking for a tail.

Thankfully, her mom had a car seat in her vehicle that Sabrina could use until she could replace hers. She would also have to replace her car or get a rental until she could. She didn't know the extent of the damage to her house but, from what she'd seen, it would be extensive. She'd worked hard to purchase a home for her and Robby and it hadn't been easy on a single mom's salary. It broke her heart that it was now unlivable. Another thing Creed had taken from her.

Jake pulled into the driveway and parked. "Want me to carry him for you?"

Robby had finally settled down on the drive and fallen asleep on her shoulder. She wanted to keep him with her but her own adrenaline rush was fading and her energy zapped. She nodded so he climbed out, circled the car then lifted Robby from her lap. Robby didn't rouse as he moved his head to Jake's shoulder instead.

She climbed out of the car and headed inside. The door opened before she arrived and her mother stood in the doorway, hand on her heart and tears welling up in her eyes. "You're both okay. God is good."

Sabrina's instinct wanted to refute her mother about God's goodness but she was just too tired tonight. Her faith had taken a hit when her brother died. Then Jake had left her. Her father's death last year had done little to make her believe any different. But she had been turning the bend again, realizing what a gift she had in Robby. What kind of a good God allowed so many terrible things to happen to one family? She didn't know but blaming God wasn't the answer. She hugged her mother. "We're okay, Mom."

Her mother released her then touched the back of Robby's head. She also touched Jake's arm. "Thank you for protecting them."

Sabrina led Jake down the hallway to the bedroom. Jake placed him on the bed then gently removed his coat, hat and boots before pulling the blanket over him. Sabrina watched as he stroked Robby's hair. His shoulders shook for a moment, then he took a deep breath and stood to face her. She recognized the firm line of his mouth as he fought for control and the what-might-have-happened fear that flashed through his eyes. He'd nearly lost something he hadn't even known he'd had earlier in the day.

He closed the door to the bedroom but didn't move from the hallway. He reached out to touch her cheek, sending chills through her. "I can't even think about what nearly happened tonight." His voice was choked, still full of emotion.

"I know. I'm glad you arrived when you did."

"When I couldn't reach you on your cell, I was worried I wouldn't make it in time." He looked back at the bedroom door and sighed. "I just found him. I can't imagine losing him now."

He leaned close and she sensed he wanted to hold her. Falling into his arms would be so easy and feel so good, yet she hesitated. That comfort would only be fleeting. Once the fear of the night became a memory, he would remember how angry he was at her for keeping Robby from him. She couldn't put herself out there only to be hurt again.

She stepped away from him and headed for the kitchen where her mom and Bob were sitting at the table. Jake followed her and, when she saw them, her mother jumped to her feet. She pulled the cell phone Sabrina had left charging from the cord and handed it to her. "Please keep this with you, Sabrina. I think tonight has proven that you never know when someone might need to reach you."

Sabrina placed it on the counter then took a coffee mug from the cabinet and poured herself a cup. It was late but there was little chance of her getting much sleep tonight after this attack.

Jake took the coffeepot from her and poured himself a cup too.

Bob motioned to the TV that was silently playing news clips. "I was just watching coverage about the police presence in your neighborhood, Sabrina. They said a neighbor noticed a suspicious vehicle and called it in and that the sheriff's office was still looking for the suspects."

She thanked him but she didn't want to hear the details. She knew who had attacked her home tonight. Her department would collect evidence and gather witness statements, but they would have a difficult time linking this attack back to Creed.

He'd taken her brother from her. Now he'd taken her home too.

She pushed the coffee away and stood, suddenly not wishing to relive this terrible night. "I should try to get some sleep. I've got that early morning meeting."

Her mother gaped. "You're not going to work tomorrow after what nearly happened tonight, are you?"

"Of course I am. I can't let Creed put me on the sidelines."

Her mother jumped to her feet. "Sabrina, why do you keep putting yourself at risk this way? You have Robby to think about."

She wasn't backing down. She couldn't allow Paul Creed to win. "I am thinking about Robby. I can't allow him to grow up in a world with drugs on every street corner. Creed is a blight on this area's good name and I won't rest until we bring him down."

Jake touched her arm. "Are you sure you're up for that? I'm sure it can wait a day or two?"

She glared at him as she pulled her arm away. They'd already had this discussion back at her house. She wasn't going into hiding. "I won't let Creed win. I won't let him stop me from doing my job. Robby will be fine here where he's safe while I do what I have to do."

"Of course I'll keep him safe," her mother assured her. "But it's not him I'm worried about, Sabrina. It's you. I've already lost a son. I can't risk losing a daughter too."

Bob reached for her mother's hand and held it then stood and pulled her into a hug. "Your mother knows how dedicated you are to your work, Sabrina, but you can't blame her for being fearful after tonight. Don't worry. I'll be around tomorrow and the next few days to make sure they're both safe. I'll even bring doughnuts when I come back in the morning. I know Robby likes the ones with sprinkles."

"Thank you, Bob. I appreciate it." She didn't particularly care for her mom's new boyfriend but was grateful he would be another eye to watch her son. She couldn't put her finger on what it was that rubbed her the wrong way, but she thought it was probably just jealousy that her mom was moving forward when Sabrina still seemed to be stuck in the past. Besides, it had only been a year since her dad had died and it felt disloyal to him to like this new man in her mom's life.

She walked down the hall to the extra

bedroom. She had some clothes and toiletries here for when she and Robby stayed over. She gathered them into a bag. She had a spare uniform in her locker at the sheriff's office but she would have to go by her house tomorrow to see what else she could salvage. The sheriff's office had cots near the jail for officers to utilize. It wouldn't grant her the comfort of home, but it was a safe option now that her house was a crime scene.

Jake followed her, his broad shoulders filling the doorway. "Are you sure this is a good idea? Creed nearly killed you tonight."

She turned and looked at him. Why did everyone insist she step back and let Creed win? "I won't let him get away with this, Jake. If I give up now, he wins."

His mouth twitched with worry. "I don't like it but I can't stop you. Promise me that you'll be careful."

"I will. I won't be alone. Besides, I can assure you that Kent will be all over me to take extra precautions after tonight." Deputy-involved shootings were treated with caution. Sabrina hadn't had time to do anything but pull her gun but she'd been a target of a drive-by shooting. Kent was protective of his deputies but he was a professional. He would appreciate her commitment to her work, but he would also admire her determination not to become a victim. At least, she hoped that was how he would react once he'd had time to think about it. He had the authority to place her on desk duty, which would be infuriating.

She was also worried about Jake. He'd risked his cover once he'd discovered the plan to attack her at home. "What will you do about Creed? Is it safe for you to return?"

"I kept my head down and my face covered so I don't think the shooters saw me and I did my best to stay clear of the news outlets. I am glad to hear that Kent put out a statement that a neighbor called in seeing a suspicious vehicle. I was worried Creed might be suspicious I'd tipped off the police given the timing, but my cover should be intact."

She hoped that was the case. She was still counting on him to help her bring down Creed and his supplier.

"Do you need a ride to the sheriff's office?"

"No. I'll call Kent and ask him to send a deputy to pick me up."

"I'll call and check on you tomorrow." He slipped her cell phone into her hand. "You left this again."

She smiled and took it. She'd left it on the counter in her haste to assert herself.

"Good night," he told her.

"Good night, Jake."

He turned and walked away and the room seemed emptier without him. She glanced out of the window, watching him as he climbed into his car and sped away.

She was grateful to him for what he'd

done tonight. She'd come far too close to losing her life and Robby's life.

Creed was dangerous and she was going to have to be on her high guard from now on.

Jake's mind was still awhirl as he headed back to the apartment, parked and got out. He was still shaking inside from the night's events. Sabrina and Robby were safe now but knowing how close they'd been to danger had rocked him. Now that his mind had time to process all that had happened, he could admit the gut punch that had come with the idea of losing them.

He didn't even know Robby. Didn't know how to be a father. But he wanted the chance to figure it out. If Creed's men had succeeded tonight, Jake's regrets would have followed him for the rest of his life.

He unlocked the apartment door then headed inside. He'd only been back in town for a few hours but those hours had changed him. He'd thought losing his twin had turned his world upside down, but discovering he was a father and nearly losing his child all in the scope of one night was too much.

And Sabrina.

He'd thwarted two attacks against her today. What would losing her again, this time for good, do to him? He didn't want to find out.

Her mission against Creed was going to be the death of her.

Jake opened the nightstand drawer beside the bed and pulled out the Bible he'd seen there earlier when he was unpacking. It had to belong to his brother. He opened it and thumbed through the pages. Max had marked up passages and made notes in the margins. Jake had been surprised to learn from Max's boss, Carl, that his brother had rediscovered his faith and was a regular member of a Bible study group when he wasn't working a job.

Jake liked that. He hadn't thought about God in years but their mom had raised them in church and the congregation they'd attended had been good to both Max and Jake after their mom died.

And, tonight, his first thought at hearing they were in danger was to call out to God for help.

A knock on the front door grabbed his attention. He slid the Bible back into the drawer and closed it, then reached for his gun as he moved across the living room floor. He glanced through the peephole, surprised by who he saw standing on the other side.

He opened the door and Creed blew past him, rubbing his hands anxiously. The man looked to be on the edge and when a notoriously dangerous drug dealer was upset, it couldn't be good. "Where have you been, Max?" he demanded. "I came by earlier and you weren't here. Where were you?"

Oh you know, just thwarting your plan to murder my ex-girlfriend and my son.

"I was just out driving around. What's the matter?"

Creed looked as if he were bordering on full-blown panic.

"My men failed to take out the deputy. They shot up her house but she managed to escape unharmed. The police were tipped off by a neighbor. I'm surprised you haven't seen it. It's been all over the local news."

"I haven't watched the news."

"My supplier is not going to be happy, Max. He wanted this done." Creed was wringing his hands and looked to be close to full-blown panic. Whoever this supplier was, he had to be one scary guy to instill fear in Paul Creed.

Jake tried to remain calm. He didn't know if Creed coming to see him was normal behavior or not since he still had no idea how much Creed had trusted Max, but he tried to play it cool. "So we'll go see this guy, your supplier, and explain. I'll go with you. He can't kill us both, right?"

"Don't be so sure." The look in Creed's face when he locked eyes with Jake showed fear.

He rubbed the back of his neck and tried to come up with another plan. "Look, this guy needs you to move his drugs. He needs you as much as you need him. Right? We'll just explain that this deputy got lucky. It won't happen again." And, suddenly, he had an idea. "What if we make an anonymous tip to the police and have these fellas that botched the hit picked up? The cops will blame them for the attempted murder and we'll blame them to the supplier for messing up the job."

Creed thought about it for a moment then shook his head. "No. They'll tie me back to the hit. They'll definitely turn on me if they believe I gave them up. I can't take that risk. That Deputy Reagan has to die. It's the only way I can save myself." He walked to the door and reached for the handle but stopped before he opened it. As he turned to say something, Jake expected a thanks for listening or something along those lines. Instead, Creed's face turned hard as he glared at Jake. "The next time I call you, you'd better answer if you know what's good for you."

He opened the door and walked off, leaving the door standing open.

Jake walked to it, watched Creed climb into his car and drive away, then closed it.

He leaned against the door and let out a deep breath.

Sabrina and Robby might be safe at the moment, but the threat wasn't over for them. Creed was even more determined than ever to kill her. Worse than that, there was some unknown figurehead supplying Creed drugs and demanding he take Sabrina's life. Even taking down Creed wasn't enough any longer. He had to find this supplier's identity to end the threat against her once and for all.

Mike Johnson was the county parole supervisor. Sabrina met up with him the next morning at the Lockwood Apartment complex Dale Lowrey had listed as his address when he'd been released from prison six months earlier. He'd been arrested along with another known associate of Creed's so she knew he was involved in the organization before he went to prison on drugs charges. Now Sabrina had received a tip that Lowrey was once again involved in the sale and distribution of drugs for Creed so she arranged to meet up with Mike to perform a search.

She'd borrowed her mom's car for the meeting until she could arrange a rental car. She parked then got out, stretching and working out the kinks from sleeping on a cot the night before. She shook hands with Mike, who was waiting for her. "Have you seen him?"

"Not yet. I parked around the corner so he wouldn't see me while I waited for you."

That was smart. If he'd been seen that gave Lowrey time to dispose of any drugs he might have in his possession. Since he was on parole, they didn't need a warrant or probable cause to search his apartment.

Johnson knocked and Lowrey quickly came to the door.

Johnson officially identified himself despite Lowrey knowing him from their monthly meetings, and Sabrina flashed her badge as well and identified herself. "We're here to perform a search," Johnson told him. "Please step back."

Lowrey didn't look happy but he didn't protest either. He knew he had no choice in the matter as part of his parole. Surprise visits were a part of his life until he was officially released from corrections custody.

They entered the small apartment and Sabrina spotted a woman and a small child in the kitchen. "Who are they?" she asked.

"My wife and daughter," Lowrey told her.

She stepped into the kitchen and identified herself. "We're going to perform a search of your apartment, Mrs. Lowrey. Are you aware of any illegal substances in the dwelling?"

She glanced at her husband then shook her head. The little girl clutched at her leg and the woman picked her up.

"Please have a seat." She turned to Lowrey. "I'm going to ask you and your family to remain in the kitchen while Mr. Johnson and I conduct the search."

"Why don't you start in the bedroom," Johnson suggested. "I'll start in here then move to the living room."

Sabrina nodded then walked to the bedroom. She clicked on the overhead light and glanced around then opened the dresser drawers and began searching. She went over the entire room and the smaller bedroom across the hall too before moving to the bathroom. She found no drugs, no large sums of cash or any drug paraphernalia. She was beginning to wonder if her tip wasn't reliable. Lowrey seemed to be keeping his nose clean.

"Found something," Johnson called to her.

She stepped into the kitchen where Johnson held up a small plastic baggie filled with pills. "I found it in the daughter's shoe by the front door. Imagine if she'd taken it to school with her."

Suddenly, Lowrey's wife grabbed the shoe, leaped to her feet and whacked her husband with it. "What were you thinking bringing drugs in here?" she screamed as the little girl began to cry.

Johnson grabbed her and pulled her

away before she could hit her husband again. "That's enough," he told her.

"It's not mine," Lowrey insisted. "I was only holding it for someone."

She'd heard that excuse before. In fact, during her time in Narcotics, she'd probably heard all the excuses. It was always someone else's fault.

"Stand up," Sabrina told him. "I'm placing you under arrest."

She drove Lowrey down to the sheriff's office and officially booked him. Then she placed him into an interview room. She let him sweat for a while hoping that he had time to think about what going back to prison would be like and hoped he would be willing to help her bring Creed's organization down in exchange for some leniency.

Once they were ready, Johnson joined Sabrina in the interview and informed Lowrey that he was going back to prison for violating his parole by having drugs in his possession. The man was nervous and kept rubbing his leg. She took that as a good indicator that he might be willing to answer her questions in exchange for a deal that kept him out of prison.

However, once she started asking him questions, Lowrey clammed up and refused to help them. She pressed him but could see the fear in his face. He was more frightened of Creed than he was of returning to prison.

"Think about your daughter," Sabrina said. She knew he'd been working during his time in prison to get straight and get back to his family but it seemed he wasn't able to keep up the straight and narrow life. "Do you want to go back to prison and not see your daughter?"

He glared at her for bringing up his child but still shook his head. "I can't help you."

Johnson stood. "That's enough. You'll go in front of a judge tomorrow at which time your parole will be revoked and you'll be returned to prison to finish out the remainder of your sentence. Your daughter will be in middle school before you see her again, Lowrey."

She walked out with Johnson, who shook his head. "I'm sorry. I really thought he might crack."

She'd thought so too. "I was hopeful but he's too afraid of Creed to talk."

That was the same brick wall she'd been hitting ever since deciding to focus on Creed. Even her own brother had been frightened of him so she understood the danger of asking these men to defy Creed, but she wasn't going to bring him down without help.

"I'll keep working on him," Johnson told her. "Maybe a night in jail will change his mind."

She thanked him but she wasn't holding her breath. She was familiar with Creed's tactics and they were intimidating.

She spotted his wife clutching the little girl sitting in the waiting area. As she signed out, the desk clerk spotted her watching them.

"They came in with Lowrey. It's his wife and daughter. She's wanting information about him."

"I know. Unfortunately, they were there when we arrested him. Let them know Mr. Johnson, his parole officer, will be out to speak with them soon."

She hated the look of disappointment and anger on the young woman's face. Another little girl would grow up without her father around and Creed was ultimately the one behind it. None of his men seemed willing to turn on him.

Her only hope now was depending on Max—Jake—to bring him down.

FIVE

Sabrina headed back for her desk and was writing up her report about Lowrey's arrest when Kent stuck his head out of his office and called for her.

She hit submit on the report then walked into his office.

He was already sitting back behind his desk when she entered. "I wanted to let you know we've identified the man who attacked you in the grocery store parking lot. His name is Lucas Davis. He has multiple arrests for drugs, assault and robbery."

She glanced through the file he handed her and shuddered at the image of the man who'd put a knife to her throat and threatened her son. "Do we have an address on him?"

He nodded. "I've already sent two deputies to the address on record but he wasn't there. I've put out a warrant for his arrest."

"Does he have any connections to Creed?"

"Nothing solid although they have known associates. Maybe he'll spill who hired him once we get him into custody."

She handed the file back to him. "I hope so."

"We're also still processing witness statements and forensics from your house but, so far, several neighbors recalled seeing a strange vehicle with several men inside. We're hoping to find video footage from security cameras to try to identify them."

She nodded. It wasn't good news. It had been dark so identifying them would be difficult but she knew Kent and the rest of her team would do their best. Jake could confirm that Creed had given the order but without knowing the shooters' identities his testimony would be worthless. "Can I go over there or is it still a crime scene? I'd like to pick up some clothes and toys for Robby."

He nodded. "I can have a deputy follow you over there and keep an eye out while you gather what you need. Then, it's probably best that you go to your mom's house and stay there."

"What do you mean?"

"I spoke with Sheriff Thompson about the attacks yesterday. She thinks it's a good idea that you take some time off and let the department handle the investigation."

Sabrina's heart sank. This was what she hadn't wanted to happen. "Why?"

"There were three separate attacks against you yesterday, Sabrina. We know from Max that Creed has placed a hit on you. It's too dangerous for you to continue to walk around like nothing happened. The sheriff thinks so and I agree with her."

Sabrina leaned across the desk. "Don't you get it, Kent? If you take me off the investigation, Creed wins."

"No, he doesn't. Max is still undercover plus this department will continue investigating. I'm adding Drake to the case. And this isn't forever. It's just until we know you're safe."

"I didn't join the sheriff's office to be safe. I joined for justice."

"I know. I'm sorry it has to be this way." He picked up the phone and called for a patrol deputy to escort her to her house. When he arrived, Sabrina, still seething, stood and headed for the door.

"I'll keep you updated on the investigations," he assured her.

She thanked him then walked out of his office. Down the hall, Sheriff Thompson's door stood open. Sabrina thought briefly about marching in there and demanding she change her mind but their sheriff couldn't be bullied. She was usually tough but fair. She'd made a decision and wouldn't be swayed. In fact, she might even call Sabrina reckless in her desire to find justice for her brother.

Sabrina walked to her desk, grabbed her keys and gun then walked to the car. She watched her mirrors as she drove but only the deputy appeared to be following her.

Her heart broke when she pulled to the curb at her home. The Christmas lights were still hanging from the eave but the front windows had been boarded up and her SUV was gone from the driveway. Crime scene tape cordoned off the lawn and driveway but Deputy Parkman removed it enough for her to pass through.

She choked back emotions as she walked through her destroyed home. This used to be her safe haven. Now she was sure they would never feel safe here again. She quickly gathered some clothes for both her and Robby. She didn't need to worry about the uniforms now but she still collected them, hopeful that Sheriff Thompson would change her mind.

Deputy Parkman kept watch as she worked then helped her load her mother's car with the items. "I'll follow you and make sure you don't have a tail," he said.

She thanked him then headed for her mom's house, taking her own safety precautions. They turned out to be un-needed since the only person following her was Deputy Parkman.

Her cell phone rang as she drove and she recognized the number.

"How are you this morning?" Jake asked once she answered.

"Not great," she admitted.

"Did something happen during your parole search?"

"We found drugs, but Lowrey is too scared of Creed to talk. Now Sheriff Thompson wants me to take some time off until this threat with Creed is over. She's basically sidelining me." She sounded like a petulant child who hadn't gotten her way but she couldn't help her frustration. The sheriff's decree was unfair. "Promise me you won't keep me in the dark, Jake, with what's going on with Creed."

He shouldn't agree to it and it wasn't right of her to put him on the spot since technically he was liaising with the sheriff's office and not just her, but she didn't want to get completely pushed out. Jake was her only connection left.

"I won't," he promised. "Creed came by my apartment last night. He was wild-eyed and acting strange. He said his supplier wasn't happy that the hit against you failed."

"I'm sorry to disappoint him."

Jake chuckled. "Me too. He didn't seem to suspect that I was involved though. I haven't seen him yet today. I'm heading over to the factory now."

"I'm glad he doesn't suspect you, Jake. I was worried he might." At least he was still able to investigate and gather evidence against Creed.

"I'm hoping I can convince him to call off the hit on you and let me handle it. If he thinks I'm targeting you, maybe no one else will."

It was a good plan. She hoped Jake could convince him. It might take the target off her back and then Sheriff Thompson would surely allow her to get back to work. "Let me know how that goes."

"I will. In fact, I was hoping I could come by later and spend some time with Robby."

She should have expected that request but it caught her off guard. Of course he would want to get to know his son and she didn't want to stand in the way of them having a relationship. "That should be fine. We'll see you then."

She ended the call surprised by the swell of emotion that overtook her. She'd known she would have to share Robby. It was the right thing to do and she certainly owed it to Jake, but the thought of sharing her son with him was scary.

She took a deep breath. She was just going to have to get used to it. Jake was a part of Robby's life now.

She parked then waved as Parkman drove off. She carried the belongings she'd gathered into the house. Her mother wasn't in sight but she passed by the playroom and saw Robby sleeping on the bed. That explained why the house was so quiet. Naptime. She dumped the stuff she was carrying onto the bed in the spare room. This would be their home for a while now and, while it wasn't his bed or his toys, at least Robby had a safe place that he was familiar with to stay. It could have been much worse.

She heard a noise and walked back into the living room only to find her mother dragging a crate across the floor.

"What are you doing?" Sabrina asked her.

"It's the Christmas decorations. I wasn't

going to put up any since Bob and I had planned a getaway for Christmas but now that you and Robby are here, I thought I should. At least for his sake."

It was just like her mother to be so selfless and think of others. It was one of the things Sabrina admired most about her mom.

She grabbed ahold of the other end of the crate and picked it up. "I'll help you."

"Don't you have to get back to work?"

"No, I don't have to worry about that at the moment." She quickly explained Sheriff Thompson's order, then helped her mom lug the remaining totes from the storage room to the living room.

It didn't take long with both of them working to put up the tree and decorate it. They stood back and admired it.

"There's still some room on the bottom limbs for Robby to add his own ornaments."

Sabrina hugged her mom. "You're the best. Thank you for letting us stay here.

I don't know what we would do without you."

"I'm sure Kent would have put you in a safe house. At least, this way, I still get to see you and Robby. Are you sure you're safe here?"

"As safe as anywhere else. No one knows where you live and since this house isn't even in your name, that helps." Sabrina's father had purchased this house from a friend of his. He'd signed the deed over but the official paperwork had never been changed. She'd pressured her mom to take care of that but, to her knowledge, she hadn't yet. "Kent also promised to increase patrols in the area but I wouldn't want to put you in danger though so if you'd rather we leave…"

"No, no, no. I was only concerned about your safety. I'm happy to have you both here. Honestly, it gets to be so quiet around here."

Sabrina understood the sentiment. Her childhood home had been full of laughter and silliness with her brother always pulling pranks and showing off. She hadn't realized back then how special her family was. Now both her dad and Robby were gone. Sabrina didn't have to deal with the quiet with an active four-year-old running around but she understood about loneliness and recognized it in her mother.

"So you and Bob seem to be getting along well. You must like him."

Her mother's face lit up with a smile. "He's wonderful. And he loves to have a good time. We go out to eat and travel and see the sights. I have fun with him."

"I'm glad to see you getting out again."

"Me too." She reached over and placed her hand on top of Sabrina's. "I'd like to see the same thing for you, sweetheart."

She shook her head, shaking away the thought. Romance was the last thing on her mind. "I've got so much going on, Mom. I don't have time to date. I have to worry about my cases and Creed, plus Robby."

"I wasn't thinking about signing you up for a dating site. You and Jake used to be quite the item. It's obvious he still cares for you, Sabrina."

She took a sip of her hot chocolate then set it down. She'd given a lot of thought to her and Jake and decided it could never work out between them no matter how much they'd once cared for each other. "That's in the past, Mom. I'll always care about Jake and he is Robby's father so, in that sense, I suppose he'll always be a part of my life. But it's also because of Robby that I know nothing romantic will ever happen between us again. You saw how angry he was when he found out I kept the truth from him. I can never make that up to him. Never."

"Yes, I remember. But I also remember how worried he was when he learned Creed had sent men to kill you."

She waved that concern away. Any decent human being would have been worried when they learned of a hit against someone, and Jake was a good person. Plus, he knew she had Robby with her. His concern might have just as easily featured his newly discovered son.

Her mom reached across a tin of ornaments and pushed a strand of hair back from Sabrina's face. "Honey, it's time you forgive yourself for not being able to help your brother. It's time for you to move on. It's time for us both to get on with our lives. What you and Jake had five years ago made you happy. I would love to see that for you again. I'm only saying not to push him away because you're afraid. Sometimes, taking a risk is worth it. Promise me that you'll think about it?"

"I will."

They'd both suffered so much after her brother's death that, for a while, she wasn't certain her mother would ever smile again. Bob Crawford had brought that back to her mom and, whatever her feelings for him, he'd brought her mom back to life again.

She stared up at the twinkling lights on the tree and wondered if she could ever feel that way again. If she did, one thing was for certain. It wouldn't be with Jake Harris. He would never be able to see past her mistake enough to forgive her for it.

Jake headed for the industrial part of town, noticing that the roads were pretty barren. This part of town had become nearly uninhabitable as more businesses shut down and moved away. It made the perfect location for Creed to conduct his business. No nosy neighbors watching what he was doing.

Jake pulled up to the gate and waved at the two men who stood guard. They opened the gate and let him through. He parked in the lot and walked inside. Creed was on the factory floor having

words with one of his foremen. Jake
didn't know his name so he avoided joining the conversation. He walked past
them to the break room and poured himself a cup of coffee.

Suddenly, a man appeared beside him,
staring him down. Him, Jake recognized.
Mick Jacoby, Creed's second in command and the source of the rumors that
Max might have been a federal agent.

"What are you looking at, Mick?" Jake
demanded. Max wouldn't kowtow to him
so Jake couldn't either.

"I'd heard you were back." He glanced
at the cast on Jake's arm. "Car accident,
huh?"

"That's right. I understand you had
your own thoughts about what happened
to me."

"Still do. I don't trust you, Max. I never
have."

So he'd been suspicious of Max from
the start. Nothing Jake could do or say
would change that, but at least he still

seemed to believe Jake was Max. "Well, I'm back now and I'm taking point on setting up a new drop-off for the next shipment."

"I've already handled that. I've got the trucks ready and waiting."

"Where's the drop-off?"

Jacoby scoffed. "Like I would tell you so you could pass it on to the cops. Besides, from what I understand, Creed's supplier won't make a move until that deputy is out the way permanently."

He walked off, leaving Jake with a conundrum. He couldn't uncover Creed's supplier until the drugs were handed off and, apparently, that wasn't going to happen until Sabrina was dead.

That meant their only chance of ending this was the flash drive he'd copied from Creed's laptop. He'd forgotten to ask Sabrina about it when he'd spoken to her but it had been less than a day since he'd given it to her. He didn't know Jana Carter, the sheriff department's IT person, but he hoped she was good at her job.

The information on that flash drive might be the only thing that could keep Sabrina alive.

"Mom, you've gone overboard again," Sabrina said as she pulled another inflatable from the crate of Christmas decorations that littered the driveway. She'd already unveiled an eight-foot snowman and now her mom had added an inflatable Santa Claus. They'd moved from decorating the inside of the house to the outside. "Your front yard is just not that big."

Her mom chuckled. "I know but I couldn't resist. Robby will love it."

She couldn't argue with that. He would love it. Something about this Christmas had changed for them and it had everything to do with Robby. Her little boy had brought such joy and happiness into their lives and driven out the sorrow and grief that had plagued Sabrina for so many years.

"I want Robby to understand that Christmas isn't about Santa. It's about the birth of Jesus."

"Will you relax," her mom told her. "I also bought a manger scene."

"There won't be room to walk on the lawn if you add all three."

She smiled. "I know. The manger scene goes on the roof."

She must have seen Sabrina's surprise because she laughed. "Don't worry. I don't expect you to climb up there. I asked Bob to come over to help. He got called away to handle some issue at his job site."

Something about her calling on her new boyfriend to save the day ruffled Sabrina's ego. "I can do it, Mom."

"Honey, let Bob get on the roof. You're supposed to be laying low, remember."

"I don't think Creed's men are going to

spot me just because I climbed onto the roof to put up Christmas decorations."

"Why take the risk?"

She walked into the garage and dug through the storage room until she found the manger scene. She dragged it, the inflatables and a crate of Christmas lights into the yard and began putting them up. A half hour later, Bob arrived. Her mother greeted him with a kiss and a mug of hot coffee. Sabrina couldn't help but see the glow in her mother's face as she talked with Bob. Her mom was falling for him hard and it was good to see her happy again. Sabrina didn't wish her mother unhappiness but this relationship with Bob had happened so suddenly and now he was all she could talk about. Sabrina didn't know if it was jealousy or a dislike of seeing her mother with someone besides her dad, but something about the man rubbed her the wrong way.

She pushed away those thoughts. She had to stop seeing suspicion in everything. She'd even done a background check on Bob Crawford and he'd checked out. No criminal history to speak of and he was active in the church and local charities. Plus, she'd never seen him be anything but attentive and affectionate toward her mother.

Bob Crawford wasn't the bad guy and Sabrina needed to stop being so cynical. She needed to get over her dislike before she ruined her relationship with her mother the way she'd ruined her relationship with Jake.

As she worked, Robby, who had awakened from his nap, ran around the lawn laughing and giggling at the inflatables. She carried the ladder from the garage to get busy hanging the house lights. She should have done this earlier in the month but her mother hadn't planned on being home for Christmas and Sabrina had been so preoccupied with Creed and worrying about Max's sudden disappearance that she'd let time slip by her. She'd promised herself that Robby would get all her attention this year and this would be his best Christmas yet and she'd already gone back on that promise without meaning to. She needed to be more intentional for her child's sake. She supposed that issue had solved itself now that she'd been ordered to take some time off.

A car pulled to the curb and Jake got out. He walked up the driveway, shook Bob's hand and spoke to her mother before walking over to where she was untangling the lights. He stopped before he reached her to kneel down to Robby and say something to him that had the little boy giggling even more and showing off the Christmas inflatables, pulling Jake by the hand to follow him.

Her heart ached at the scene. Father and son enjoying a happy Christmas moment. Tears pressed against her eyes as she realized how much Jake had missed and it was because of her that he had.

She'd robbed him and Robby of that special time that they could never get back. How could he ever forgive her for that?

He played with Robby a few more minutes but the moment she stepped up onto the ladder, he rushed over to her. "Do you want some help with that?"

"I can handle it. I've strung lights before." She'd hung her own house lights with no help. A lot of good that had done her.

He put his hands on the ladder. "I don't mind, Sabrina."

"I appreciate it but I'd much rather see you with Robby. It was nice."

He looked back at Robby and a smile filled his face. "I liked it too. He's so excited about Christmas."

"Yes, he is, and I want to make this his best one yet."

"I want that too."

She reached to string a line of lights and reached a bit too far, causing the ladder to wobble. Jake steadied it but Sabrina lost her balance, falling backward. She screamed but Jake caught her before she hit the ground.

"I've got you," he said.

As she stared up into his blue eyes, she was stunned at the way her pulse raced and the electricity between them. From the look on his face, he felt it too.

Her mother and Bob came running, breaking the spell over them. "Sabrina, are you all right? I told you not to climb up that ladder."

Jake set her down and she tried to shake off the headiness from being in his arms. "I'm fine," she insisted. "I just tumbled. It was dumb. I should have moved the ladder."

"Honey, you're bleeding."

She lifted her arm and saw a gash on her forearm. She hadn't even felt it but it was bleeding badly.

"I'll get a towel," her mother said then dashed inside.

Jake took her arm and held it up. "Keep

the wound up so it won't bleed as much. You must have clipped it on the ladder."

"I didn't even feel it," she said, her face warming as she realized she was too busy falling into his lovely blue eyes.

"That looks deep. You might need stitches," Bob stated.

Jake agreed. "I'll drive you to the emergency room."

Robby, seeing the commotion, came running up to her. "Mommy, are you hurt?"

"I'm okay, baby. Just cut myself. I'm going to go see the doctor to take care of it while you stay here with Grandma and Bob and finish the decorating."

He seemed okay with that once he knew she wasn't seriously injured.

"I'll finish hanging these," Bob offered but Jake stopped him.

"I can do it when I get back. I don't mind."

They argued for a few minutes over who would finish the light hanging until her mother returned with a towel and pressed it against her arm.

"I don't care who hangs them but someone needs to take my daughter to the hospital."

That seemed to bring Jake to his senses. "I'm driving her."

"Good, then Bob can finish the lights. Make sure she's safe."

"I will," he promised her.

Sabrina walked to the car with Jake's hand at her back. She was thankful he was there and for the comfort he provided. She still wasn't feeling much pain but the bleeding was still heavy and she could see for herself that stitches might be needed.

He made the drive to the hospital in record time and parked near the entrance to the emergency room. As he helped her from the car, she realized she was feeling a bit lightheaded, probably from the blood loss.

"I'm right here. Lean on me," he said and, for once, she didn't argue.

They walked inside and Jake planted her into a seat then walked to the counter and registered her to be seen.

"You don't have to stay," she told him as he slipped into the chair beside her. "I appreciate the ride but you don't have to stay."

"I'd prefer it if you don't mind."

She shook her head then stared off. She would have never believed that something as simple as talking to Jake Harris would be difficult, but she couldn't seem to find the words to speak to him. She wasn't looking for a fight but she also wasn't interested in discussing why she'd been so affected by his arms around her either.

It was getting harder and harder to make believe that he didn't still have an effect on her. That her knees didn't go weak at his touch or his smile send her spiraling like a silly schoolgirl on her first crush.

Jake Harris was not a crush. He'd been her first love. Her first everything until she'd pushed him away. She'd deprived him of knowing he had a son and that was something unforgivable. No use in losing her heart to him when he would never reciprocate. She'd missed her chance at happiness when she'd allowed grief to send her to a dark place.

She had no right to fall for him again.

The towel she'd pressed against her wound had bled through. Thankfully, the emergency room wasn't busy and they were able to send her to a curtained-off area quickly.

Jake paced as the nurse cleaned her wound then announced she would need stitches. "How did you manage to do this?" she asked Sabrina.

"I was hanging Christmas lights and fell. I guess I cut it on the ladder."

The nurse quickly stitched up the gash

then arranged for her release. "My supervisor will have to come in and check on you and give the okay to release you. Once he does that, you'll be free to go."

There was little to do except sit back and wait for that to happen. She watched Jake standing by the curtain, peering out periodically to keep an eye out. She appreciated his being with her and doing what he could to keep her safe, but she realized he'd come to the house to see Robby, not to help her. "I'm sorry I'm taking away your time with Robby."

"It's okay. I'm sure he'll feel better knowing that his mom is okay."

He was probably right. After the attack at the house last night, she was surprised Robby hadn't clung to her leg or cried when she left. The trauma had to have affected him. He was one tough little kid.

Jake peered through the curtain again only, this time, his shoulders tensed.

"What is it?" Sabrina demanded, sitting up.

"I can see the outside entrance from here. Two of Creed's men just showed up."

She tensed too and hopped off the gurney, pulling on her jacket, and glanced over his shoulder. Sure enough, two men had entered the area and were glancing around.

"I don't recognize them. Are you sure they work for Creed?"

He nodded. "Definitely. I saw them last night at the factory."

"Do you think they're searching for me? How would they know I was here?"

He rubbed the back of his neck. "I'm not sure but we should get out of here before they see us."

She agreed. Waiting around would do them no good and they didn't want a confrontation with these men in the hospital. It still bugged her though that they were here. It couldn't be a coincidence, could it?

"I should call Kent and alert him."

She reached into her pocket for her cell phone but it wasn't there. She clearly remembered sliding it into her back pocket earlier in the day. It must have dropped out when she'd fallen from the ladder. "I don't have my phone. Let me use yours."

He started to reach into his pocket to retrieve it, but stopped. "We should go now. They're rounding the check-in desk."

Sabrina peeked out from behind the curtain and realized he was right. These men were in search mode and she and Jake were sitting ducks.

They slipped through the curtain and down the hallway to an emergency door that opened directly to the back area of the hospital which housed the labs and diagnostic equipment. Only employees were generally back here. Patients were usually escorted. Thankfully, she knew her way through the hospital, having run emergency drills last year as part of a crisis readiness response with the county and state law enforcement agencies.

She led him through the hallways until they were deep inside the building. There was a back door through the cafeteria's kitchen that led outside and that was where she was headed. They needed to get away from these men before they were seen, then call Kent to send backup.

Jake's heavy breathing and footfalls pressed her forward. They weren't running yet but they moved quickly through the building toward their destination. Her eyes scanned her surroundings and the people they passed, on alert for any evidence of their being discovered.

She heard rattling as she darted through a doorway and turned to see the two men appear at the end of the hallway. Only a locked set of doors kept them from approaching but she could see their faces through the glass inserts. They'd found them.

"This way." Jake pushed her through the doorway into the kitchen area.

She felt him pressing her to go faster

and she darted around the personnel and equipment toward the back door. She burst through it into the cold night air but didn't slow down.

"Keep going," Jake insisted.

Her pace didn't slow as she ran across the parking lot. Jake's car was parked on the other side of the medical center building but it was too dangerous to try to reach it with these men on their trail. She darted across the street to a grassy area with an embankment instead where Jake grabbed her arm and pulled her to the ground, taking cover behind the hill. Her heart was pounding and they were both out of breath but she was glad for the respite. She peeked over a hill at the door they'd just run through, watching and waiting to see if they'd been followed.

Sabrina's breath was visible on the air and the chill of the night rolled over her. She rubbed her arms, gasping when she hit the area with the newly treated gash.

"That was close," she said but she spotted a worried expression on Jake's face. "Do you think we lost them?"

He let out a breath which she could see hanging in the air. He shook his head and she followed his gaze. The doors opened again and the two men exited the building and scanned the area, guns in hand. The duo locked eyes on their position then rushed their way.

He pulled his gun from its holster. "Did you bring your weapon?"

She shook her head. She hadn't brought anything—purse, ID, cell phone—when she'd left the house. Of course, she hadn't planned on needing any of that stuff when she was putting up Christmas decorations. Now she regretted that decision.

Shots rang out. They were firing and it was two guns against one. Getting into a gunfight now wasn't the smart move unless they were cornered.

"Let's get out of here," Jake said. "Try

to make it to the shopping center across the way."

She couldn't agree more. They had to find a way to lose these armed gunmen before they caught up to them. The shopping center in the distance was a good idea. Even Creed's men wouldn't dare open fire around so many people...she hoped. It should provide them with cover and a place to hide and call for help.

But, first, they had to make it there alive.

SIX

Sabrina didn't let up as they darted across a median and down a hill. Jake turned to glance behind them. Their pursuers were still there, doing their best to catch up before Jake and Sabrina made it to safety.

If she'd had her gun on her they might be able to stop and engage them but he couldn't take them both on alone. Getting to safety was their best chance of survival.

They reached the parking lot of the shopping center. Thankfully, it was lit up with Christmas lights and bustling with shoppers. Sabrina darted through the crowd and took cover in a vestibule that had a sign pointing to the restrooms so he followed her. They pressed themselves against the wall and crouched down, trying not to attract attention.

"Give me your cell phone," she instructed. He handed it over and she dialed a number. "I'll have Kent send a car and a patrol team to flush these guys out."

It was a good idea. Patrol officers could apprehend or at least distract the assailants while Sabrina and Jake got away. He was hoping too to keep his identity hidden.

If that still even mattered.

"They're on the way," Sabrina told him.

She fidgeted with her arm and panic filled him. He moved closer to her to examine her wound. "Were you hit?"

"No, it's just sore where the stitches are." She looked at him and her brows creased with worry. "Are you hurt?"

He shook his head. "No."

"Then what's the matter?"

He started to protest that nothing was wrong but she cut him off before he could speak.

"I know you, Jake. I've always been able to tell when something was bugging you. Now, what's wrong?"

He couldn't help a smile at the truth in her statement. She had always been able to read his emotions like a book. "It's probably nothing but those men might have seen me."

"Sure, they saw us both."

"I mean, they might have seen my face, Sabrina. If they know who I am then my cover might have just been blown."

"Oh." He saw the consequence of that settle on her face. "But you don't know if they did."

He shook his head. "I don't know for certain. I can't be sure how good of a look they even got of me."

She reached for his hand. "Then we'll worry about that later. For now, we're safe." Sirens sounded and patrol lights lit up the night as two sheriff's office cruisers pulled up to the curb. "Here's our ride."

Sabrina got back on the phone and co-ordinated with the patrol officers to clear out an area so that she and Jake could jump to a vehicle without being seen. "Take us to the station," she ordered the deputy behind the wheel once they were safely inside the patrol cruiser.

By the time they arrived at the sheriff's office, Kent was waiting in his office along with Sheriff Deena Thompson. It was the first time he'd met her so he reached to shake her hand and she reciprocated.

"Are you all right?" Kent asked Sabrina first thing.

She nodded. "I'm fine." She motioned to stitches on her arm. "I cut myself while I was putting up Christmas lights and Max offered to drive me to the emergency room. That's when Creed's men arrived. We had to leave his car behind at the hospital."

Kent nodded then picked up the phone. "I'll have someone go retrieve it." He made the call and Jake handed over his keys to the deputy who arrived to go get the car from the hospital parking lot.

Once they were gone, Sabrina turned to Kent and the sheriff. "Those men might have blown his cover."

"How certain are you?" Sheriff Thompson asked Jake.

He rubbed the back of his neck and sighed. "I'm not sure at all if you want to know the truth. I saw them from behind the curtain at the hospital and they might have seen me from behind but we were running and hiding so they might not have gotten a good look at my face. Even if they did, I can't be sure they know who I am."

"What do you want to do?" Kent asked.

"I should at least find out."

Sabrina's mouth fell open. "What are

you talking about? You can't go back there. Creed will know you're working undercover."

Jake understood her concern but how could he walk away from this investigation if there was a possibility that his identity hadn't been compromised? He owed it to his brother to at least make sure before he gave up. And he still needed to keep her safe.

Sabrina looked at Sheriff Thompson. "You can't let him go back in there. It's too dangerous."

Sheriff Thompson glanced at her then at Jake. "It's not my place to tell him what he can and can't do. Technically, this isn't our investigation. It's the DEA's. Maybe you should call your supervisor and talk to him about what you should do."

That was a good idea and he might do that. Carl would probably advise him not to risk it, but Jake wasn't willing to give up so easily. If his cover was still intact, he wasn't walking away from completing the mission his brother had started. Besides, with the target on Sabrina, flushing out Creed's supplier was now all the more important. If he could do that from the inside then it was the better option.

He glanced at Sabrina. He understood her concern but he'd given her the courtesy of knowing what was best for her. He hoped she would do the same.

"My real concern is how Creed's men knew you were there," Kent stated.

Sabrina shrugged. "I have no idea. I find it hard to believe they followed us from my mom's place. I made sure I wasn't followed there when I left my house this afternoon."

Unfortunately, Jake had an idea of who might have tipped them off. "I had a run-in today with Mick Jacoby. He doesn't trust me. It's possible he had someone following me and that I led them there." He found it difficult to believe he hadn't noticed a tail, but it wasn't impossible that was what had happened. If that was the case then his cover had surely been compromised. Going back in was a risk but it was one he had to take.

Kent glanced at Sheriff Thompson then back at Jake. "Whether or not you go back in is your call."

Jake made a decision. "I'll go back to the apartment and phone Carl and talk it over with him before I decide anything."

Sabrina folded her arms and he could see she wasn't happy with his decision. He didn't want to anger her but he couldn't just walk away. He owed it to Max and he owed it to her. As long as she was in danger, he had to do everything he could to stop Creed.

Sabrina was quiet on the drive back to her mom's house, which was fine with Jake. He was glad to have his car returned but he was extra careful to take precautions and check his mirrors for a tail as he drove. He still found it hard to believe that he could have missed one following him to Sabrina's house, but he had no other way of explaining how they'd tracked her to the hospital. They made it to the house without being seen. He stopped at the curb, noticing the lights were up and on. Bob must have finished hanging them as he and Sabrina were running for their lives. Through the front window, he spotted Beverly, Bob and Robby in the living room.

She saw it too. "What's going to happen to Robby if you get killed, Jake? You just found out you have a son and you want to take this big risk? Why would you do that?"

"You didn't like being told to back off the investigation, did you?"

Her face reddened at that admonishment.

"Creed is dangerous, Sabrina. He's placed a target on your back. As long as he's out there, I can't leave."

She reached for his hand. "Please just think about this, Jake. I know you want to bring Creed down. So do I. But think about your son. He needs his father." She leaned over and kissed his cheek, then hopped out and ran inside.

He made sure she was in before he drove off. He headed back to the apartment then had second thoughts. If his cover was blown, Creed's men would be waiting for him there. He had a lot to think about and he wasn't sure what to do. He wished there was a way to know whether or not his cover had been compromised before he placed himself in Creed's path. Confusion had set in. He'd come to town with only one mission—to finish Max's undercover job. Now everything had gotten so muddled.

He parked at the apartment building and scanned the lot and buildings. He didn't see anything out of place but his instincts were on alert. Something was wrong. He started the car and peeled out instead. He headed down the road, unsure of what to do next. He could return to the sheriff's office and admit the operation was over or he could risk his life to find out if his cover had been blown.

He turned back around. What he'd told Sabrina was right. He had to take the risk. He parked then headed up to the apartment and approached the door. He was still watching but if someone was out there, they were doing a good job of hiding themselves.

He unlocked the door and pushed it open.

Suddenly, his neighbor's door opened and someone grabbed him from behind, shoving him into the apartment. Another figure ran at him with a baseball bat and slammed it against his head before he could reach for his gun.

Jake slid to the floor as agonizing pain ripped through him and darkness filled the edges of his vision. One of the men grabbed his arm and flipped him over and he saw it was the same two assailants who'd chased them from the hospital.

"Mr. Creed said to bring you in," one of them stated, and Jake was helpless to fight back as unconsciousness pulled him under.

Jake's first realization as he regained consciousness was that he was no longer at his apartment. He opened his eyes, pain ripping through his head at the light. He moaned in pain then jerked when he tried to raise his hand to shield his eyes. Both hands were tied to a chair. He pulled at his feet. They were bound too.

He glanced up and spotted one of the men who'd attacked him.

"You're awake. Good."

"Why am I here?" He figured he knew the reason but he needed to continue with his cover until he knew for certain it had been blown. "Why did Creed send you after me?"

"I just follow orders. We'll know soon enough. He's on his way here."

As he finished speaking, the door slid open. Jake braced himself, only it wasn't Creed who entered. It was the other one of the duo who'd overpowered him.

"Where's Creed?" number one asked his partner.

"On his way." He cracked his knuckles. "But, first, let's have some fun and tenderize this guy for him."

He punched Jake, sending him and the chair to the floor. Jake was riddled with pain at the punch and the sting of his back, arm and head as he hit the floor. The two men pulled him back up for more beatings. They weren't done with him yet.

Suddenly, someone shouted and the men calmed then moved aside. Creed stepped forward with several other men, including Mick Jacoby with a smug look, standing behind him. He folded his arms as he stared at Jake. "How long did you think you could fool us? You're playing both sides."

"I don't know what Jacoby said to you—"

"This isn't about what he said or didn't say, Max. You were seen by Ethan and Dax here helping that Deputy Reagan escape the hospital. You're helping her which can only mean that you aren't who you say you are. Are you working undercover?"

So Creed's men had seen him at the hospital and recognized him. That explained the abduction and beating. Creed thought he'd been betrayed. He had been, but if Jake could convince him otherwise then the case could still be salvaged.

And he had just the idea.

"It's not true," he told Creed. "I'm not working undercover and I'm not helping Deputy Reagan."

Jacoby stepped forward. "My men saw you with their own eyes. Are you calling them liars?"

Ethan and Dax nodded. "Yeah, we

saw you," one of them—he didn't know which—said.

He looked at Creed. "You don't understand. I have a twin brother—Jake. He and Deputy Reagan were an item back in the day. High school sweethearts. I'd heard he was back in town to see her. It must have been him your guys saw."

"They said it was you," Jacoby insisted, running at Jake and punching him in the face.

Jake tasted blood but didn't give in to the pain. "We're identical twins. They probably wouldn't have been able to tell the difference between him and me."

Creed chuckled and turned to his men. "Identical twins. Sure, Max. You're really going to try to play the twin angle. How dumb do you think I am?"

He wasn't dumb but it helped that Jake wasn't lying about being a twin and could even prove his claim. "We both played ball for Mercy High School and we were good. There's a display at the high school with our picture, standing side by side on the basketball court. That will prove to you that I'm telling the truth about being a twin."

Jacoby looked ready to pounce on him again, but Creed stopped him. He appeared intrigued. "What's your brother's name?"

"Jake—Jake Harris. He's a detective with the San Antonio Police Department. The department can also confirm his existence."

"You have a twin brother who's a cop?"

"Yes, I do. We went our separate ways after college. He chose law enforcement and I chose another direction. He was always the good guy and I was the one who didn't like to follow the rules." That part wasn't true. Max had been the more determined one of the two of them. Jake had found a place in San Antonio PD while Max was always taking risks and working his way up the ladder. Working undercover had been a natural fit for him because he was charismatic and fearless while Jake had always been the more cautious one...at least until now.

"If you don't believe me, go to the high school and look at the display. I know it's still there because I saw it a few days ago. Go see that then come back and call me a liar again." He was daring them to do his bidding but he had to put up the bravado in order to sell his story. These men wouldn't easily be fooled but, this time, his story might sound reasonable. Max had bragged about their photos still being displayed when they'd met up.

Creed considered it for a moment then nodded. He motioned to Ethan and Dax, who cut Jake's binds then forced him to stand.

"You're not actually believing his story, are you?" Jacoby asked Creed.

"We're all going together to verify your story," Creed told Jake. "That way, if I don't believe it, we won't have to drive far to dump your body."

They led him outside to the car then shoved him into the back seat and pushed him into the middle. Ethan sat on one side while Dax took the other. Jacoby didn't look happy as he climbed into the driver's seat but Creed, who took shotgun, didn't seem to care.

Jake took advantage of having access to his hands to touch his jaw where he'd been hit more than once. The physical pain stung, sure, but he was thinking what would happen if they didn't believe this story. If he couldn't talk his way out of this mess, these men would kill him. He didn't want to die but, more than that, he didn't want to abandon Sabrina. He'd give anything for one more chance to see her. He wasn't ready to die today.

They reached the high school and Dax used a crowbar to pry open the front door. Ethan grabbed Jake's arm and walked him down a long hallway to a display case near the front office, following behind Creed and Jacoby.

Even in the dark hallway, the trophy case was backlit and the honors and displays were visible. Creed bent over and looked hard at the photo of Jake and Max front and center on the basketball team. Their team had won the championship that year. Another photo of just Max and Jake showed them at homecoming. Sabrina was on Jake's arm in that photo and their names were listed which only served to further prove his story about he and Sabrina being high school sweethearts.

He glanced at the photo and the smiles on both their faces. He'd known even then how much he'd loved her. He hadn't even been able to imagine a life without her. And it had been just as empty and lonely without her as his teenaged self could have ever imagined.

Creed straightened. "I'll be. Even side by side, I can't tell the difference. It's creepy."

It wasn't the first time he'd heard that

sentiment. He usually didn't care for it but he wouldn't argue about it today. "So then you believe me?"

Creed thought for a moment and looked at the photos again before finally nodding. "I guess I do. Your story checks out. You do have an identical twin brother named Jake Harris. The only question that remains is whether or not he's in town." He took out his cell phone and dialed information. "San Antonio Police Department and please connect me."

Jake waited as the call went through and Creed asked for him by name. Several moments passed before he ended the call and slid the phone back into his pocket.

"What did they say?" Jake asked him, praying for good news.

"That Detective Jake Harris was out of town on personal business."

Good. One of the DEA's demands for Jake taking over the investigation was that his chief had had to sign off on the assignment too. Thankfully, he'd agreed and promised to run cover for Jake's absence. It seemed that had paid off now. "Now do you believe me?"

Creed again thought for a moment before nodding. "Let him go."

The goon squad released him and Jake rubbed his jaw, still stinging from the beating.

Only Creed wasn't done. "The fact that your brother is in town and helping Deputy Reagan puts him in the line of fire. You realize that, don't you? If he gets in the way of our target on Deputy Reagan, it could get him killed."

Jake nodded, understanding Creed's meaning, but he had to keep up pretenses. "Like I said, we aren't that close. If he's in town to see her then he won't hesitate to step in to protect her." He meant those words even if Creed took them to mean something different.

"Let's go."

They walked away, leaving Jake standing at the display case and on the hook to find his own way back. That was fine with him. He was just glad to see them walking away from him instead of walking him to some ditch to execute him. He'd managed to talk his way out of this one but he doubted Creed would trust him after this even if he did believe the story. There were too many suspicions around him now to let him back into the trusted circle. The case was compromised but not completely dead yet. He just needed to find the information about Creed's supplier sooner rather than later.

He stared at the high school photos in the case and all those memories came rushing back to him. Him and Max. Him and Sabrina. The three of them had been nearly inseparable and he'd never imagined a time when neither one of them weren't in his life. Now Max was dead and he'd lived years without Sabrina. Not one day had felt right to him either without her by his side. Leaving her had been the biggest mistake he could have made and he was determined to do whatever it took to make it up to her and Robby, even if it meant stepping into the line of fire to protect her.

He walked outside and headed down the road. It was a long, cold walk back to his apartment building but what else could he do? He didn't have his cell phone and pay phones were nonexistent these days. He rubbed his arms to warm them up, wishing Ethan and Dax hadn't waited until he'd shed his jacket to attack.

Headlights lit the dark street heading his way. He shielded his eyes but was glad to see it. Maybe he could flag down the car for a ride or, at least, use the driver's cell phone.

Instead of slowing, the car sped up, darting toward him. Jake jumped out of the way but the car swerved, hitting him and sending him reeling. As he slammed against the pavement, the car skidded to a stop, the door opened and someone got out.

Jake tried to push himself up but the figure approaching put his boot on Jake's back and pushed him back down.

"Creed may have believed your story, but I still don't trust you," Jacoby told Jake as he pulled his gun. "And I'm determined to find out the truth."

SEVEN

Sabrina cooked up a pan of scrambled eggs and sausage then loaded it onto a plate and placed it in front of Robby. He dug into the meal but his attention was mostly on the kids' show playing on the television on the kitchen counter.

Usually, they would be heading out to preschool at this time of the morning but with the holiday season and the risks to her life, Sabrina was glad they had nowhere to go today. She pushed Robby's hair from his face. Maybe a break from her job and spending the day with him wasn't the worst thing in the world.

But her mind wasn't far away from Jake either and worrying about what he was going to do. She prayed he wouldn't try to go back to Creed's. It was just too dangerous and he wasn't ready to lose him. She glanced at Robby again. Jake had a son to think about now. He couldn't take unnecessary risks.

She picked up her cell phone and called him. The phone rang several times before sending the call to voicemail. "Hey, it's me. I'm wondering what you decided. Call me back."

She kept herself busy and tried to phone Jake several more times with no response. That worried her. If he'd gone back in with Creed and his cover was fine, he might not be able to answer her or call her back. She couldn't even think about the other alternative.

Finally, her phone rang and she scrambled to answer it, but it wasn't Jake. "Kent, hi."

"I wanted to let you know that I checked in with Jana about the flash drive. She's still working on breaking through the encryption. I'm asking Agent Price if the DEA's technical team can assist."

She sighed. It looked like that flash drive might be a dead end unless Jana could find a way to break it. Asking for help was the smart move. With Jake's cover blown, she'd been hoping that might identify Creed's supplier. "Thanks for the update. Hey, Kent, have you heard from Max?"

"No, I haven't. I take it you haven't either?"

"No. When I left him last night, he was still trying to decide what to do. I was hoping he would call me this morning."

"I'm sure he'll check in soon. Another reason I was calling is that the court clerk phoned. She's missing some paperwork on the Dale Lowrey case and the judge wants you to give him an account of the search of Lowrey's apartment. He's claiming Johnson planted those drugs."

She shook her head. "That didn't happen. Mike Johnson is too honest to do something like that."

"Well, the judge is expecting you at the courthouse in an hour. I'm sending Deputy Parkman to pick you up and take you. I don't want you driving around alone."

She ended the call then changed into her uniform. Thankfully, her mom was home to watch Robby since judges didn't care about babysitting issues.

She tried phoning Jake again as she waited for Deputy Parkman to arrive. Still no answer. Now she was starting to get worried. This wasn't like him.

Parkman arrived and Sabrina dashed out and got into the passenger seat. "Thanks for the ride, Tim."

"No problem. Commander Morgan instructed me to make sure you weren't left alone. I'm to remain with you at the courthouse then drive you back home."

"After I see the judge, before you drive me home, I have one more stop to make. I need to go by and check on a friend."

He nodded then drove her to the court-house. She was glad to have Deputy Parkman watching her back, but she was still on alert herself as she entered the courthouse. She went in front of the judge and explained what had happened in the Lowrey case, including the anony-mous tip she'd received and her estima-tion of Johnson's character. She hadn't been in the room when he'd found the drugs but she had worked with him pre-viously and known him to be an honest and forthright man. It wasn't uncommon for prisoners to accuse law enforcement of planting evidence and, given Low-rey's drug history and known associa-tion with Creed, Sabrina had no doubt that the drugs had belonged to him.

The judge agreed with her assessment and revoked Lowrey's parole, sending him back to prison to complete his sen-tence. Sabrina watched as his wife and daughter cried then hugged him before he was removed from the courtroom to return to jail. He'd made a decision to do something that would take him away from his family so it was difficult for her to feel sorry for him.

However, it made Sabrina wonder if Jake had also made a decision that might have taken him away from her and Robby.

She climbed back into the car with Deputy Parkman then gave him the address of Max's apartment complex where Jake had been staying. They pulled into the parking lot and she immediately spotted Jake's rental in a parking spot. Her heart skipped a beat at seeing it. If his car was here, why wasn't he answering his phone or responding to her calls?

Deputy Parkman parked and they got out and walked up to the apartment. She knocked but heard no movement from inside. The door was locked so they walked down to the manager's office and had them open the door. Sabrina's mind was whirling with what they might find.

Was he lying unconscious or dead inside? It was the only thing that explained why he hadn't returned her calls.

The manager opened the door and Deputy Parkman stepped inside first. Sabrina held her breath as she glanced around. Jake wasn't there. Parkman checked the bedroom and bathroom then shook his head.

"He's not here."

"When was the last time you've seen Mr. Harris?" she asked the manager.

"I don't usually. I live on the other side of the complex. He pays his rent online and hasn't had any maintenance issues since moving in."

"I don't see any evidence of a struggle," Parkman noted and she couldn't argue. Jake was just gone.

"Lock this place back up," she told the manager then walked outside to the car.

"Where to now?" Parkman asked her. "Home?"

"No." She couldn't shake the idea that

something terrible had happened to Jake. He'd been out of contact with her for too long. "Take me back to the sheriff's office. I need to speak with Kent."

They drove back to the sheriff's office and Sabrina immediately marched into Kent's office. "I'm worried about Max. I haven't heard from him since last night."

Kent leaned back in his chair. "Was he supposed to check in with you?"

"No. We didn't have anything planned to check in but he's been in touch with me often since he's been back in town. Now it's radio silence. He's not answering his phone, he's not returning my calls and Deputy Parkman and I went by his apartment and he's not there either even though his car is sitting in its parking space. I'm worried, Kent. He might have tried to go back to Creed's factory and been taken."

"Max has always been able to take care of himself," Kent reminded her. "Plus, he knew the danger when he accepted this assignment."

She bit her lip. She didn't like keeping this secret from him. He still didn't know Max wasn't Max, and she wasn't sure if she needed to tell him now that he wasn't checking in.

"That's just it, Kent. I don't know that he can." She'd seen Max's capabilities and never worried about him, but she wasn't falling in love with Max Harris either. She'd seen Jake stand up to Creed and his men and step in to protect her, but she had no idea how he would do in a pinch or how well he could think on his feet. She trusted him but she wasn't sure she trusted him not to get himself killed. He was determined to finish the investigation for Max's sake and also to keep her safe.

Kent stood. "Look, he disappeared once before. He doesn't work for us so technically we have no control over his comings and goings. Sure, we made an agreement to give him backup if needed and in exchange, he would provide us with information, but we can't jump to conclusions without proof. If he needed help, he would have reached out. We don't know anything is wrong yet. It hasn't even been a day."

She'd zeroed in on his words though and they'd bit at her. "You think he might have just left town?"

He shrugged. "It happened before, then he showed back up after weeks with little to no explanation. I know you want Creed brought down and, I agree, Max is our best chance of that happening but we don't control him. He's free to leave whenever he wants. Last night, he wasn't sure whether or not his cover had been blown. It's possible he decided it was and just left."

She tried her best not to let Kent see how his words had impacted her, but his reminder was like a gut punch. She turned and left his office. Now she was worried, but not about Jake's safety, because Kent was right without even realizing it. Jake had left her before. He'd walked out of her life five years ago and she had no assurances that he wouldn't do so again. The thought of that nearly doubled her over. She found a quiet corner and sat down, putting her hands over her face. She tried to breathe and push away her doubts about Jake. He might leave her, and she couldn't blame him, but he'd expressed an interest in getting to know Robby. He wouldn't leave his son. Not on purpose.

She pulled out her cell phone and tried his number again. No answer. Panic rose in her. Something was wrong. She felt it in her gut.

She walked back to her desk and dug through her notes until she located the name and number for Max's supervisor, Carl Price. She should run this through Kent first but even he didn't know about Jake. Aside from her, only one other per-

188 Dangerous Christmas Investigation

son knew the truth about him and he might have the answers she sought.

She walked outside for privacy then dialed the number for Agent Price of the DEA. When he answered, she introduced herself.

"I'm Deputy Sabrina Reagan of the Mercy County Sheriff's Office."

"Deputy Reagan, what can I do for you?"

"I'm calling about Agent Max Harris." She sighed, realizing there was no point in beating around the bush. "I'm calling about Jake."

"Jake?" He sounded stunned at the name. "I'm not sure who—"

"I knew it was him and not Max the moment I saw him but, don't worry, I'm the only one who knows."

He breathed a sigh of relief. "What about him? Why are you calling?"

"I think he might be missing. I haven't heard from him in hours and that's not like him. I'm worried that his cover might have been compromised."

"That is worrisome. How long has it been since he's checked in?"

"I haven't heard from him since last night. I was wondering... I mean, you haven't heard from him, have you? He hasn't let you know that he's abandoning the mission and going back to San Antonio?"

"No, I haven't heard a word from him. I confess, I've been waiting on a check-in myself."

"How long does he need to be missing before I start searching for him officially?"

"Let me make some calls and see if I can hear anything. I'll call you back."

She walked back into the squad room. She wouldn't rest until she heard something back from him. The fact that Price hadn't heard from him either didn't ease her mind. She was even more certain that something had happened to him.

Allison, the dispatcher walked past her desk and Sabrina heard her speak with Kent. "We have a reported break-in at the high school from last night. I sent patrols but they're asking for someone from investigations. Who should I give it to?"

Sabrina glanced around, realizing that all the desks were empty. Everyone else was out on calls. She hurried into Kent's office. "I'll go," Sabrina stated. Anything to get her mind off Jake and wondering why he hadn't returned her calls.

Break-ins were often also tied to drug crimes so it was a natural thing for her to cross over into burglary work. However, she didn't know what could be happening at the high school unless someone had left drugs in their locker.

Kent shook his head. "You're not supposed to be out in the field. Sheriff's orders, remember?"

"I'll be surrounded by deputies the entire time," she reminded him. "I'll be safe. Plus, everyone else is tied up with another case."

He rubbed his chin, considering it then gave the okay. "Make sure Parkman goes with you."

It was a compromise she was willing to accept.

Deputy Parkman drove her to the high school. Once there, she found the responding deputies were still on the scene. "What do we have?" she asked the lead one.

"The front entrance doors were broken in and we have footprints leading down the main hallway. They lead right to the front office but it doesn't look like the office was broken into. Those doors are still locked and it doesn't appear that anything was taken that we can see. I've contacted the principal who is on his way down here to confirm that."

She walked inside and spotted the multiple shoe prints that lined the main hallway. This was more than one person.

And the prints were different sizes and marks. She counted at least three distinct ones. As the lead deputy had stated, they went straight to the office then stopped and turned back. Odd that they didn't seem to pass by anything of value. A few more steps into the office and they could have gotten computers, laptops, cameras and other valuable equipment.

A deputy approached her leading another man. "This is Principal Jackson. This is Deputy Reagan," he said, making introductions.

Sabrina shook his hand. "Thanks for coming down. If you could check the office or look for anything that might be missing that would be great."

"We have cameras set up around the office. I can get the video footage."

"Thanks. That sounds great." Cameras had made her job a lot easier in some ways. She hoped this would be one of those times.

He nodded then unlocked the office and started looking around.

As she walked around, Sabrina noticed the glass trophy case. She looked inside, startled to see a photo of Jake and Max on the basketball team along with one of her and Jake and Max and a date on homecoming. She smiled at the memory. Simpler times.

The principal returned with his cell phone out. "Nothing appears to be missing. In fact, I looked through the video feed and it doesn't look like they even entered the office."

"Kids?" she asked.

"No. Adult men." He handed over his cell phone and she pressed play on the already cued-up video.

A group of four men, two in the front and two following behind, walked into view but like the principal stated, they stopped at the office doors. They turned to look instead at the glass trophy case.

She zoomed in on the faces and gasped

at the recognition. It was Jake and he looked beaten and bruised. She recognized one of the other men too as Paul Creed.

But why would they come here to look at a trophy case?

That's when she realized. Jake must have shown them the images of him and his brother. Something had happened and he'd needed to prove he was a twin. Had they discovered he wasn't Max after all?

Her mind spun at what must have happened.

She pulled the lead deputy aside. "I want you to start a search of the school grounds and let me know if you find anyone." She didn't know what they'd done with Jake after they'd left. Had he convinced them or had they killed him and dumped his body?

She phoned Kent and updated him on seeing Jake on the video. "Creed definitely has him and he looked to be injured. We need to find him."

It was enough to convince him. "Don't worry. We will find him."

She hurried outside and joined in the search. She tried his phone again but it was still going straight to voicemail.

"Where are you, Jake?" she whispered to the wind. "And are you safe?"

She wasn't letting Kent send her back home again until she knew the truth.

Jake pulled at the ropes tying his hands and feet. He was tied up and lying on the dirt floor of a place he recognized. The old sawmill in Harper Woods. He and his brother and Sabrina had spent time in these woods as kids as had many of the other kids they'd known. This old sawmill had been the optimal place for parties and hanging out.

Now it was his prison.

He glared up at one of the men standing watch over him. He couldn't remember if that was Ethan or Dax. It didn't matter. Both of them were just pawns in this sick game.

"Why am I here?" Jake demanded. "Creed said he believed me."

Obviously something had gone wrong between the time Creed had let him go and Jacoby had grabbed him.

"Creed might believe you but Jacoby doesn't. He's keeping you out of the way until he can figure out what you're up to."

"I'm not up to anything," Jake insisted.

He'd known Jacoby didn't trust him but he hadn't expected this. He'd talked his way out of Creed's distrust but Jacoby hadn't been convinced.

He didn't know exactly how long he'd been here but, as he watched the sun set through the windows of the sawmill, he knew it had been at least a day. Sabrina must be going out of her mind with worry. He hoped he could get back to her soon.

He heard tires outside. His captor heard

it too and got up and glanced out the window then moved to open the door.

Jake hurried to sit up. He'd been trying to wiggle or break his binds all day but Ethan or Dax, whoever he was, had been checking them periodically.

The doors swung open and Jacoby walked in with the other half of the duo and Creed following behind him. "How is he?" Jacoby demanded.

"Still locked up tight," Ethan told him.

They moved toward Jake so he went on the offensive. "What is this? What's going on?"

Creed paced in front of him like a caged animal. "I trusted you. That's what's going on here. I let you into my operation and all the while you were spying on me."

"That's not true. I told you my brother—"

Creed stopped him. "I know, I know. It was your twin. Here's the thing."

Creed motioned to Jacoby, who pulled out his laptop and opened it up. A video was already keyed up. Jake swallowed hard when he saw it security feed from the hospital.

"Notice anything?" Jacoby asked him but didn't wait for an answer. He pointed to the screen. "It's clear to see that the man who helped the deputy escape from the hospital is wearing the same exact clothes as you."

Jake cringed at that video. He hadn't had time to change clothes and hadn't thought any more about it. Obviously, Jacoby had. Jake glanced at Creed. He seemed to believe it too.

"But wait, there's more," Creed said. "The night you showed back up in town, I wanted to believe your story but I had to be sure after the rumors so I sent someone to that city where you had your accident. I had someone go to the hospital and start asking questions. He cozied up to one of the aides and started asking about a car wreck. She remembered it. Said it was two brothers, twins. They were both cops. She also remembered that someone from the DEA was there. And that one of the brothers never left the hospital. He died from his injuries."

Jake did his best to conceal his shock. Creed had done his homework and, although HIPPA laws should have prevented anyone from talking, there were always slip-ups. Especially when someone dies and it's covered up. People notice.

He'd hoped they'd been far enough away from where the accident had happened that that kind of information wouldn't make it back to anyone here in town, but he should have known Creed was smart and careful. After the mix-up with him being seen with Sabrina, he'd hoped he'd talked his way out of being discovered but he'd only been fooling himself.

"Only one of those brothers made it out of that wreck alive," Creed continued. "Now, I don't know if you're Max or if you're really his brother or not, but I now know that, whoever you are, you're a cop who has infiltrated my operation. That's something I can't overlook."

Jake pulled at the ropes again and knew he was in trouble. Sabrina had been right about him not following up. He probably should have laid low after nearly being discovered before but he'd refused to leave her. He'd wanted this investigation over and done with and Creed and his supplier behind bars so he could build a future with Sabrina and Robby.

"Creed—"

He cut him off again. "I don't want to hear any more of your lies." He turned to his men. "Take him out to the woods and take care of him. Then head over to Deputy Reagan's house and take care of her too. I'm tired of these games. I've got business to see to." Creed turned and walked out.

One of the goons walked over and pulled out a knife. Jake tensed, thinking he was about to get stabbed but he used it to cut Jake's binds on his feet. However, they left his hands bound together. Each one of them grabbed him by the arm and pulled him to his feet. They took him and walked him outside to a car. Jake spotted Creed climbing into an SUV with some other men then driving away. Ethan opened the trunk to another car and Dax shoved Jake inside as Jacoby watched. They slammed the trunk, closing him in. Moments later, they climbed inside and started the car.

As Jake listened to the hum of the tires on the pavement, he knew he had to think of something or else he was going to die tonight. He wasn't ready to say goodbye to Sabrina and he wanted the opportunity to see his son grow up and become a man. He'd just discovered he was a father. He wasn't ready to end that now. He had to do something.

He searched the trunk and found a sharp piece of metal, which he used to cut at the ropes around his wrist. It took a few minutes but it sliced through the rope and also through his arm. He grimaced but couldn't do anything about that at the moment although he ripped off a piece of his shirt to use as a makeshift bandage.

His pulse shot up as the car stopped and the engine shut off. They were here, wherever here was, to the place they meant to kill him. If he didn't make it through the next few moments, he would lose everything and Sabrina might not ever know what had happened to him.

Would she wonder if he'd left her again? That would almost be worse than her believing he'd been killed. He never wanted to hurt her that way ever again.

As he grabbed the metal and braced himself for the fight of his life, he heard footsteps approaching. When the trunk opened, he acted, kicking the hood up so that it slammed against Ethan's head. He stumbled backward while Jake jumped from the trunk and tackled Dax, knocking him to the ground too. Before they could get back up, he darted into the woods. He heard shouting but kept running, taking safety in the camouflage of the trees.

He didn't know where he was but he was determined to get back to Sabrina and Robby no matter what.

The two men must have quickly recovered because gunshots fired at Jake as he ran. He had no idea where he was or how he was going to get away but his only thought was to get back to his family.

He'd known coming into this that it would be dangerous but he hadn't been thinking about Sabrina when he'd agreed to it. He'd only been trying to honor his brother by finishing this investigation. Now there was the real possibility that he might die because of it.

He pushed through branches and over-grown weeds. The gunfire ceased but he didn't realize it until he stopped and listened, realizing they were no longer shooting at him. They wouldn't just let him go though. They would be coming searching for him to end his life.

Lord, please let me get back to Sabrina. Help me through this.

He ran again. Darkness covered everything. The only light was from the moon above but he couldn't let that stop him. These men were dangerous and would be coming after him. He had to find a way to safety before that happened.

He stopped and crouched behind a tree to catch his breath and listen. He heard nothing except the sounds of chirping and humming of the night woods. No footsteps or rustling of leaves. Good. Maybe they'd gone another direction and weren't on his tail.

Then another sound caught his ear. Something else. He sat and listened until he realized what it was. Traffic.

He headed toward it, praying it remained. He must be close to the highway and hopefully he could flag down a car to help him. He ran and finally pushed out of the brush and onto the side of a road.

Headlights headed his way. Remembering how Jacoby had run him down, he hesitated only a moment. He had no choice but to take the risk. He darted up an embankment and into the road, waving his arms to flag down the car.

It slowed then stopped in the middle of the road and the driver rolled down the passenger window. Jake stumbled backward for a moment, wary of it being one of Creed's men but he couldn't think that way or he would never find help.

"Your car break down?" the man asked him.

"I was attacked," he replied. "I need to get to town to the sheriff's office. Can you take me there or call them for me?"

The driver's face registered shock then his eyes looked Jake up and down, his gaze focusing on the bloody bandage on his arm, the cast on his other arm, and the cuts and bruises on his face. He nodded and unlocked the door. "Get in. I'll drive you to town."

Jake thanked him then climbed into the passenger seat. As the man drove away, Jake leaned against the seat and sighed. He'd made it. He'd lived through being abducted by Creed's men.

He was going to see Sabrina and Robby again.

EIGHT

Sabrina went to the ladies' room and splashed her face with water.

The terror of seeing Jake beaten and bruised and being led around by Creed and his men had confirmed her worst fears. Jake's life was in danger. But it wasn't that truth that had sent her hiding out. It was the doubts about him that she'd allowed to creep into her mind. That Jake had left her again just as he had five years earlier.

She had done her best to push them away but they'd managed to keep popping up and breaking her heart. She should never have doubted him.

She composed herself, then walked back into the squad room. Kent, along with Sheriff Thompson and Deputy Josh Knight, who was the head of the department's SWAT team, were going over scenarios for rescuing Jake. Thanks to Max, they knew the location of Creed's base, the old factory on the industrial area of town, but they had no confirmation that Jake was being kept there. They couldn't breach the factory until they knew for certain where Creed was holding him.

Lord, please keep him safe until we can find him.

She surprised herself with that silent cry for help. God hadn't been there for her when her brother and her dad had died. Why would He help her now?

Kent turned to look at her, regret shining in his face that he hadn't trusted her earlier intuition that something had happened to Jake. He motioned her over to join in on the planning. It was already late in the evening but the office hadn't slowed. They were already hours behind that video and each moment that they didn't find Jake was another hour of uncertainty.

"I'm putting together a team to survey the factory," Josh was telling them. "Once we have confirmation that Agent Harris is there, we'll wait for the signal to breach the factory." Josh was a former Navy SEAL and had built the department's SWAT team from scratch. He was currently focusing on training duties since being injured in a confrontation with a suspect but he was the most experienced tactically that the Mercy County Sheriff's Office had.

Sheriff Thompson looked over his suggestions then gave her okay. "Let's be careful on this. I've been in touch with Agent Price at the DEA and he's offered assistance in case we need it."

"They're not going to help?" Sabrina asked her.

She shook her head. "Agents understand going in undercover that they risk being captured. They're trained to think on their feet and take risks. The agency is still concerned about preserving the operation and discovering Paul Creed's supplier. He plays a much bigger role in the drug trade around the state and country."

"So they're just willing to sacrifice one agent in order to preserve their operation?" Sabrina couldn't imagine working for an agency that wouldn't intervene to rescue one of its agents when they were in trouble.

Sheriff Thompson must have seen her horror. She took Sabrina's arm. "The DEA is a big agency with a lot of red tape. I believe Agent Price cares about Max and will do what he can for him. In the meantime, we'll do what we can do."

"Thank you, Sheriff."

The sheriff turned back to Kent and Josh. "Keep me updated. I'll be in my office."

Suddenly, Allison rushed into the room.

"Commander, we just received a call in dispatch about Agent Harris."

A buzz of excitement filled the room but Sabrina's heart fell and fear gripped her. "What was it?" she asked, fearful of the answer to the question even as she asked it.

Allison's face spread into a grin. "A motorist just picked him up on the side of the road. He'd been beaten and nearly killed but he's alive, Sabrina. He's alive."

Sabrina jumped into her embrace and Allison hugged her back. She could hardly contain herself. "Where is he now?"

"The driver is bringing him in. I sent a cruiser to intercept them. Apparently, he stumbled out of the woods near the old sawmill."

She breathed in a sigh of relief and fought back tears. He was alive. *Thank You, Lord, for bringing him home again.* Maybe God was listening after all.

She watched the door and listened to the radio, her leg bouncing nervously until she spotted the cruiser pulling into the station. She ran to the door and saw a car behind it. The passenger door opened and she spotted Jake lean over and say something to the driver before shaking his hand. Then he got out.

She ran to him, circling the car. Even from a distance, the outside lights illuminated blood on his face and clothes and he looked like he'd been through the wringer.

He saw her too. "Sabrina."

She pressed herself against him and his arms circled hers, pulling her in tightly. A swell of emotion threatened to overtake her but she finally managed to speak. "Don't you ever leave me again," she told him.

He leaned back and looked at her, smiling, then grimaced at the pain of the action. "Never again. That's a promise."

That was a promise she would make certain he would never break.

* * *

Jake leaned against Sabrina as she helped him inside. He'd been so frightened that he wouldn't see her again. Now he was here, safe, with her by his side.

"Call for an ambulance," Sabrina called out as they entered the station.

"No," Jake insisted. "I don't need to go to the hospital. I'm fine."

She touched his busted lip, causing him to grimace. "I can see you're not. You need to be seen by a doctor."

She wasn't wrong, but still he protested. "I took a beating, that's for sure, but I'm not seriously injured." He would have been if he hadn't fled. He'd been only moments away from getting a bullet to the back of his head. But he hadn't been shot. He touched her face. He was safe now.

She must have seen the determination in his face because she nodded. "Fine, but you need to sit and at least have a paramedic look you over." He started to protest again but she cut him off sternly. "I insist on that or I call for the ambulance."

He knew that look of determination in her eyes. It had been a long time since he'd been on the other end of it. He smiled at the memory. She'd always been a fierce protector of those she cared about. "Okay," he finally agreed.

She nodded to a woman who picked up the phone and called for a paramedic. Sabrina led him into a conference room. A couch sat on one end and she gently helped him down into it. His ribs ached as he lowered himself. He didn't think they were broken, bruised maybe, but not broken, yet she still shot him a glare of agitation.

"I'm fine," he assured her again. "I will be fine."

The door pushed open and the sheriff entered followed by Kent.

"I'm glad to see you're safe," Sheriff Thompson said.

"Thank you."

"Can you tell us what happened?"

"After I left you all the other night, I went back to my apartment. Two of Creed's men were there waiting for me. They knocked me out and tied me up."

"So they did recognize you from the hospital," Sheriff Thompson stated.

Jake nodded. "Yes, they did. I thought I had talked my way out of it. Creed seemed to believe me for a moment but then one of his men who never trusted me much obtained the video feeds from the hospital and they realized I was wearing the same clothes as the man at the hospital. I hadn't even had time to change."

"What about the break-in at the high school? How did that play into it?"

Jake glanced at Sabrina. She gave him a slight shake of her head confirming she hadn't told them about him taking over his brother's identity. They still believed he was Max and it was too complicated to explain at the moment. "It was a ploy. I tried to convince them it was my twin brother they'd seen at the hospital helping Sabrina. We went to the school so that I could show them our high school pictures proving that I had an identical twin."

They seemed to accept that explanation which was good because he wasn't up for a full-blown interrogation. His head was pounding and his ribs ached, making it difficult to breathe, much less talk.

Sheriff Thompson turned to Kent. "Let's get an arrest warrant for Paul Creed."

Jake also gave them the names of Mick Jacoby along with Ethan and Dax. "I don't know their last names but they're the ones who abducted me and kept me tied up."

Sheriff Thompson nodded and Kent strode away to make it happen. "We're already working on a plan to breach the factory. If we can't get Creed on drug charges, at least we'll be able to imprison him for kidnapping and attempted murder."

That would still leave Creed's supplier at large but it would have to be enough for now and hopefully that would alleviate the threat against Sabrina if Creed and his men were in custody. And, who knows, one of them might even crack and name the supplier. That was the best case scenario. "Thank you, Sheriff."

"My pleasure. You should give your boss a call too. He needs to know you're safe."

She walked out and left them alone and he turned to Sabrina. "You called Agent Price?"

"You've been missing for almost thirty hours, Jake. When I couldn't get in touch with you, I was hoping he'd heard from you."

So she'd thought he might have left her. He probably deserved that.

"I should call him and let him know you're safe."

She got up and pulled out her cell phone. He was glad to hand that task over to her as the pain in his rib cage intensified.

He hated that she ever thought for a moment that he would have left her. He would spend the rest of his life making certain she never doubted him again.

"I'm glad to hear he's safe," Agent Price said through the phone after Sabrina had let him know Jake had returned. She hated to phone him so late, it was nearly midnight, but knew he would want to be informed. "I hope he doesn't have any plans to confront Creed again."

She shuddered at the thought. "I'm planning on keeping him away from Creed."

"Good. Take care of him," Price told her. "I'll check in on him soon."

Sabrina ended the call then stared into the conference room at Jake. Price had encouraged her to take care of him and that was exactly what she planned to do.

Her fears about losing him when he'd vanished had proven to her how much she'd started to care for him again. She'd pushed him away five years ago and now she knew how much she regretted that decision.

Kent exited his office and called her name. "Can I talk with you for a moment?" He closed the door behind her as she entered then motioned for her to sit down as he circled back around to his chair. He looked tired and worn out from lack of sleep just as they all were.

Instead of sitting, he folded his arms and stared at her, giving her the feeling of suddenly being called out by the principal.

"Is something wrong, Kent?"

"You haven't exactly been acting like a coworker where Max is concerned. When he went missing, you were upset and panicked. Now that he's back..." he hesitated before continuing "...well, it's obvious your relationship is something more than just professional. When were you going to tell me that you and Max have been seeing one another?"

Her face warmed at being called out for her unprofessional behavior. She couldn't dispute his observations because he wasn't wrong. She and Jake were much more than deputy and DEA agent. Somewhere along the way since he'd returned to town, their relationship had turned. "It's not what you think."

"Isn't it? You practically flung yourself into his arms the moment you saw him. Look, Sabrina, I don't begrudge you happiness. In fact, I've never seen you like this, but you have to know it breaks every protocol we have."

"I know."

"How long has this been going on?"

She stared at him and knew that, as long as she was coming clean, it was time he knew the real truth. "Years ago, I dated Max's brother, Jake. We were high school sweethearts planning a future together. At least, we were until my brother died. I didn't handle my grief so well and I pushed Jake away. It was only after he left town that I discovered I was pregnant with Robby."

Kent rubbed a hand through his hair then sat down.

"I sent Jake a letter telling him about Robby but I never heard back so I assumed the worst about him but when Max arrived back in town to start this undercover operation, he figured it out and knew his brother hadn't gotten that letter. He wanted me to tell Jake the truth but I never could get up the courage."

"Okay, that still doesn't explain how you and Max—"

"Max died three weeks ago in a car crash. That's why he vanished so suddenly. He drove out to meet up with his brother and he was killed."

Confusion clouded his face. "I don't understand. How—"

"I guess I forgot to mention that Jake and Max were twins. Identical twins."

Understanding dawned on his face and he leaned back in his chair. "Identical."

"Yes. The man who came back to town wasn't Max. It was Jake. He and Max's boss worked out some scheme so that Jake would pretend to be his brother and finish the undercover operation he started. The funny thing was that no one knew the difference. Not you. Not even Creed. But I could always tell them apart when few others could."

"So the man who has been hanging around for the past week has been Jake? Agent Price sent a civilian in to Creed's operation?"

"No, of course he didn't. Jake is a cop too. Plus, he's had experience working undercover."

He nodded then looked at her. "And he's Robby's father and your ex?"

She nodded. "Yes. I'm sorry, Kent. I

should have told you sooner but it wasn't my secret to tell."

"And this newfound affection between the two of you?"

"That was unexpected. I never thought I would see Jake again and, if I did, I figured he would never forgive me for not telling him about Robby. He still might not. I don't know what our future holds but I know when I couldn't reach him, when he wasn't responding to my calls and I was afraid Creed had discovered he was undercover, I couldn't even think straight. I couldn't imagine my life without him in it."

Kent stood and walked around the desk. He put his hands over hers. "I'm sure I wasn't the only one who saw the chemistry between the two of you, Sabrina. It's obvious he cares for you too."

Something in her chest fluttered at the idea and she couldn't stop the smile that spread across her face. "I hope you're right. I don't want to lose him again, Kent."

He walked back to his desk, opened a drawer and pulled out a set of keys which he handed to her. "My uncle-in-law has a cabin out near Deer Lake. I'm sending you the GPS coordinates. Since I know you don't have a car here and you won't want to use a marked cruiser, borrow one of the cars from the impound lot and take Max, uhm Jake, to the cabin. He can use it as a safe house. Now that Creed knows he's a cop, he needs to stay out of sight. Creed's men will be searching for him to finish the job they started."

She shuddered at the thought of his life in danger and how he'd barely escaped them.

"He can hide out there until he's healed, then we'll figure out what to do. I'll be in touch with his—Max's—supervisor and update him."

"Thank you, Kent."

She turned to walk out but he called

her name and she stopped at the door to turn back to him.

"Sabrina, be careful you're not followed. It's awfully isolated out there and there won't be any backup if they find him."

She nodded then walked out and made the arrangements for a car to be made available for her. Once that was done, she hurried into the conference room where a paramedic she recognized was bandaging Jake's ribs. "I don't think he has any broken ribs as far as I can tell," he told Sabrina. "But he needs to be in a hospital and have an X-ray to be sure."

"They'll heal," Jake assured him, dismissing that idea. He must have sensed her hesitation because he pushed himself to his feet. "I'll be fine. I don't need a hospital."

"Are you sure?"

He nodded then leaned against her. "I'd be too exposed there. I just need to get somewhere safe where they can't find me then I'll be okay."

She carefully put his arm over her shoulder so he could lean on her. "I have just the place. Let's go while it's still dark outside and before Creed's men realize you came here. They'll be looking for you."

He nodded and accepted her help to walk out to the car. He slid into the passenger seat while she drove.

"Where are we going?" he asked once they were on their way.

"To an isolated cabin on Deer Lake. It belongs to someone in Kent's family. He gave me the keys." She gripped the steering wheel. "I told him, Jake. I told him everything."

He reached for her hand and she took his. "It's okay," he assured her. "We're going to need all the help we can get."

She nodded, knowing that was the truth. Now that Creed knew about him, he would send his men after them both.

She was already a target and, now, Jake had become one too.

Now that Jake had been outed by Creed, he needed a place to lay low and recover from the beatings they'd inflicted on him. Sabrina was thankful that Kent had offered this place for him to stay.

She gripped the steering wheel as she drove toward it, her emotions threatening to get the better of her. She'd been so worried about him but also had her doubts about whether or not he'd left on his own. She was ashamed of that now. She should have trusted that he would never leave her and Robby without a word.

She drove for over an hour, stopping only for gas and groceries at a small convenience store, then searched the dark, isolated streets until she found the turn-off for the cabin. She got out and unlocked the gate that blocked the entrance, insisting that Jake stay put when he tried to get out to do it. She pulled the car forward then closed it behind them as she followed the long road that led to a clearing and a small cabin. She glanced around, spotting lights in the distance but not too close. It was isolated which was good. No curious neighbors would be wondering why he was laying low. She unlocked the cabin door then switched on the overhead light, thankful the place was wired for electricity but she would need to build a fire to run out the chill in the air.

She helped him inside then settled him on the couch before making a fire in the fireplace. Now that the adrenaline had worn off, he was moving slowly. She'd insisted he needed to be in a hospital but he'd refused to go, assuring her that he was sore but not badly injured.

"Let me fix you something to eat," she said as she retrieved a bag of groceries from the car. She'd stopped at a small convenience store once they'd cleared town and she'd determined they weren't being followed. They hadn't offered many options but she'd managed to find the necessities. She popped open a can of soup and poured it into a boiler on the stove. As she waited for it to heat up, she grabbed the bandages and got to work making certain his wounds were clean.

He grabbed her hand and squeezed it, causing her to look up into his eyes. He put his hand around her neck. "I'm fine, Sabrina. I promise."

"I was so worried about you when I didn't hear from you. I just knew Creed had done something to you. I was so afraid I would never see you again." Her voice cracked with emotion and she cleared it away.

He touched her cheek. "I have to admit, all I could think about was getting back to you and Robby. I didn't want to die and leave you alone. And I never wanted you to wonder if I'd just left you again."

She glanced up at him, wondering if he

could see the doubts in her face. "How did you know?"

"I didn't. I just kept thinking that's what you might believe. You obviously did."

"Only for a moment, then I realized the truth that you wouldn't do that."

"Even though I did once before?"

She sighed and replaced the bandage on his arm. "That was different, Jake. I pushed you away. I was a mess."

He touched her face again. "And I was foolish. I should have fought harder for you. I should never have let you push me away. I promise you it will never happen again, Sabrina. I don't ever want to be without you again."

He leaned in and kissed her and she melted into his embrace. All their past baggage seemed to vanish in his kiss. It was both exciting and new and familiar and comforting.

"I'd better check on your soup."

She stood and walked to the stove. Her

knees were still shaking from that kiss. Her world had been changed in one moment when she'd thought she might not see him again and it opened up something in her. She wanted to be with Jake. She wanted him in her life and she wanted Robby to know him. He was a good man that she'd let slip through her fingers once. She couldn't let that happen again.

She turned off the stove and emptied the soup into a bowl. She turned around and he was behind her, touching her hair, and every inch of her wanted to fall into his embrace.

He kissed her and she kissed him back.

The world vanished around them during that kiss and she knew only one thing—she didn't want to be without Jake in her life again.

They sat by the fire talking and dozing for hours as the sun rose outside the window. She glanced at her watch. She needed to get back but she didn't want to leave him. "I'll fix you some breakfast then I really should go."

He pulled her back down for one more kiss. "Promise me you'll be safe."

She touched his face. "I will. Promise me you won't leave this cabin for anything."

"I won't even stick my head out the door. I promise."

"Good. I don't want anything to happen to you, Jake. I want you to stick around and spend Christmas with me and Robby."

He stroked her face and smiled. "There's nothing I want more than to be with you both."

She scrambled some eggs and made coffee and Jake managed to make it from the couch to the table to eat. Only, he hardly touched his breakfast.

"What's the matter?"

"I was just thinking about the mission. It's over now. I know that. I can never go back. Creed may not realize I'm not Max, but he knows I'm law enforcement."

She nodded. "That's true. Your cover is blown."

"I feel like I've let you down."

"You haven't."

"I was supposed to come here and finish what my brother started. I couldn't do it. I failed him and I failed you too."

She shook her head. "No, that's not true. You did the best you could."

"I'm not going to be able to bring Creed or his organization down. I didn't even find out who his supplier was."

"Don't worry about that. We'll figure out something else. We still have the flash drive you got. Jan is still working on cracking that."

He shook his head. "You don't understand. As long as he's still out there, as long as he's still in power, he's a threat to you, Sabrina. He sent men to kill you. He's dangerous and I couldn't do anything to stop him from coming after you."

She appreciated his concern for her but she'd been a target before he'd even arrived in town. This wasn't his fault. "This isn't over, Jake. I'm still determined to make him pay for what he did to my brother. I won't stop."

She saw concern spread across his face. "I don't like you being out there and me stuck here unable to do anything to help you."

"You came back to me. That's all the incentive I need to keep going. Now, at least, we can try to charge him for abducting you."

He shook his head. "That won't hold up. Creed is smart. He'll have his men testify that it never happened and I can't prove I was there."

She realized he was right. "At least all the lying is over now and I don't have to pretend you're Max. It's been so hard keeping that secret. I want the world to know how much you mean to me. How much you've always meant to me, Jake."

ing rob them both of years of being together and of him being in Robby's life.

"I'm sorry," she told him.

"About what?"

"I should have told you right away
when I discovered I was pregnant. It was
wrong of me to keep Robby from you all
these years."

He brushed a stray hair from her face.
"I confess I was hurt when I found out
he was my child but I'm not angry about
it. I understand how it happened. I'm just
glad to know that Robby helped you get
past all that with your brother. I wish
it could have been me that helped you
through it. I should never have left you,
Sabrina. For that, I'm sorry."

She was glad to hear him say that and sad for all the years they'd lost.

A ding from her cell indicated she had a text message. She pulled out her cell phone and glanced at the screen. "It's from my mom. She took Robby to the park and wants me to meet them there." The message included a photo of Robby laughing on the swings.

She showed it to Jake, who smiled. "Looks like he's having a good time."

"He loves to swing."

Jake stared at the image then smiled. "When I saw him the other day laughing and running around those inflatables, it made me realize what I was fighting for."

"I know. Me too. We'll make this the best Christmas he's ever had, won't we?"

He nodded. "Yes, we will. Together."

She kissed him again then grabbed her things. "I'll try to come by later this evening to fix you something to eat."

"You shouldn't. I can take care of myself. Besides, it's too risky. Someone might follow you here."

"I know how to watch for a tail," she assured him. "But I understand your concern. Promise you'll call me if you need anything?"

He nodded. "I will. I promise. But I'll be fine."

She still didn't want to leave but she had to think of Robby. If her mother was wanting her to come, she might need some help with him.

She got back into the car and headed toward town to the park but her mind wasn't far from the kiss she and Jake had shared. She was still reeling from it and from the near miss they'd experienced.

Nothing like nearly dying to make you realize how much you care about someone.

She reached the park and turned in. She could see the playground from the parking lot and it was full of kids running around, laughing, playing, swinging. This place was always busy during the day but Robby loved coming and it worked off some energy for him.

She spotted Robby climbing up the slide and called his name. He turned and waved to her with a big smile.

"Watch, Momma!" he yelled then slid.

She clapped and cheered him on. "Good job, baby," she said as he immediately spun and turned to climb back up and do it again.

Sabrina spotted her mother sitting on a bench on the other side. She had a book in her hand and hadn't noticed Sabrina yet until she approached her. "Hi, Mom."

She looked up then smiled and closed the book. "Sabrina, what are you doing here?"

What was her mother up to? "What do you mean? You asked me to stop by."

"No, I don't think I did."

"Mom, you texted me a photo of Robby on the swings and asked me to stop by the park." She pulled out her phone and showed her the message.

"I—I didn't send that." She dug through her own purse and pulled out her cell phone.

"What do you mean?" She took the phone and scrolled through her mom's messages. The texts she'd received weren't there. "But I—"

Suddenly, dread filled her. She scrolled through her mom's images saved to the camera but didn't see the one she'd received either. Someone else had been taking photos of Robby. Someone else had sent that message asking her to come.

She spun around to put her eyes on Robby. She couldn't see him but tried not to panic. That didn't mean he wasn't inside the play place climbing back up to the slide. She circled the structure but didn't see him.

"Robby!" Her voice screeched his name. People stopped and turned but she still didn't see Robby. She climbed up into the playground structure and checked every slide and ladder and nook and cranny for him. Nothing.

She hopped off, praying he'd gone to the swings but he wasn't there either.

"My little boy, he's gone," she told the adults she spotted. "He's got dark hair and was wearing a red jacket."

Another mother stopped her. "Are you okay?"

"I can't find my son. Robby!" she screamed again as panic ripped through her.

Now her mother was up looking too and calling his name. Several of the parents had joined the search and were also calling his name.

One woman grabbed her shoulder and pointed near the parking lot. "Is that him?"

Sabrina spun around to see a man carrying a little boy in a red jacket. He was sprinting across the grass toward a van waiting in the parking lot right by her car.

Her heart sank and she took off after him. "That's my son!" she shouted to him but the man only ran faster. She was hardly to the grass when he hopped into the van with Robby and slammed the door. The van sped away carrying her baby inside.

She wouldn't let that stop her. She ran to the car only to find two of her tires flat. She took out her cell phone and took photos of the van as it sped out of the park and onto the main street.

When it was out of view, she crumpled to the grass as sobs racked her body.

Robby had been abducted.

NINE

The sheriff's office arrived quickly and processed the scene but Sabrina was too stunned to participate in asking questions or gathering evidence. She'd given a statement to Deputy Mike Tyner, who was the first investigator on the scene and handed over the photos of the van speeding away but that was all. She could usually pull herself together and do what needed to be done in stressful situations, but this was her child, her baby, that they'd taken from her.

A car stopped and she spotted Jake getting out of the back seat. He was moving slowly but he was here and she was thankful for whomever had given him a ride. He'd promised not to leave the cabin; however, when your child had been abducted things changed.

She stood and ran to him and he circled his arms around her as she pressed her face into his chest. He grunted as if it hurt him to move that quickly but he didn't release her.

"What happened?" he asked after holding her in silence and letting her cry for several moments.

"There were at least two of them. One grabbed Robby and threw him into the van. Another was driving. They sent me this photo and lured me here to watch." She handed the cell phone to him and he glanced at the image then his jaw tensed.

"This says it came from your mom's phone."

"She didn't send it, Jake. I checked her phone. She didn't send it and she didn't have this photo of Robby. They were watching him, ready to snatch him up."

"And they wanted you here to see it happen."

She'd thought the same thing. "They have our baby."

He glanced past her and she turned and followed his gaze to her mother sitting back on the same bench where she'd been, only now she was surrounded by deputies peppering her with questions.

He walked that way and she followed along with him.

"Did you notice anyone paying extra special attention to Robby today or any other day?" Mike asked. He held a notebook in his hand and was jotting down notes.

"No. I didn't see anyone." Mrs. Reagan glanced up and locked gazes with Sabrina. Tears filled her eyes. "I'm so sorry, honey. I should have been paying more attention but I didn't see anyone."

Her first instinct was to lash out. Her mother had been reading and not paying attention to Robby, but she bit her tongue. This wasn't her fault. She knew exactly who was to blame for this.

Deputy Lisa Patterson pulled her and Jake aside. In her hand, she held her mom's cell phone and an evidence bag. "I'm going to take this back to the lab and see if someone can decipher what happened. We'll look for fingerprints although your mom insists she had the phone in her purse the entire time and didn't leave it alone for a moment. Only someone must have sent those messages then deleted them."

"There is another possibility," Jake said. "The phone could have been cloned. It's obvious whoever did this meant for Sabrina to be here to watch the abduction happen. They sent that message then waited for her to arrive. They wanted to torture her with it."

She grimaced. "And we all know who wants me to suffer."

Creed had had her son kidnapped.

"Well, I'm not going to sit around here and wait for him to act. I'm going after him and getting Robby back."

Jake grabbed her arm to stop her. "And do what? Burst up into his factory with nothing more than indignation. Do you really think Robby will be there? We have to be smart about this."

"What are we supposed to do besides just sit here and do nothing?"

"We wait. He did this for a purpose, Sabrina. He wants something from us. He'll contact us and I don't believe he will hurt Robby. He needs him to get to us."

"No. I won't sit around waiting, Jake. I'm going to find my son. We know where Creed's operation is located. I'm going there."

"No, you're not." She turned and saw Kent heading her way. She hadn't seen him earlier so he must have just arrived. "I can't let you do that either, Sabrina. Look, I've got eyes on the warehouse for now and there is no sign of Robby. Jake is right. Creed needs him alive but he knows his operation is compromised. He's probably got him holed up in a motel room or someplace like that and we're checking everything. Believe me, finding Robby is a priority for all of us."

Another car parked and her mom's boyfriend got out and ran up to the marked off area where a deputy stopped him. Sabrina spotted him and waved him through. He hurried over and hugged her mom, who fell apart into his arms.

"Is there any update?" he asked, glancing at Sabrina.

"Not yet," Jake told him. "But it's still early. The sheriff's office is doing everything they can."

He nodded. "Of course they are." He tightened his grip on her mom. "I'll take you home," he told her.

As they walked past, her mom stopped and reached out her hand to Sabrina. "I'm so sorry, honey."

Sabrina turned away. She still couldn't look at her.

"This is not your fault, Bev," Jake told her. "Just give her some time."

They walked off and Sabrina watched them climb into Bob's car then disappear down the road.

"That wasn't very kind," Jake scolded her.

She knew it wasn't and she didn't mean to blame her mom but her emotions at the moment were so raw. "I can't worry about her feelings right now, Jake. I just want my son back."

Kent finished conferring with his deputies then walked back toward her and Jake. "We've interviewed all the families that were here today and no one saw anything unusual. I'm going to release them but we've got everyone's contact numbers plus we've documented all the license plate numbers of the vehicles in the lot. I've also issued a BOLO for the van and we're trying to get tech to see if they can enhance those photos you took and see a tag number. I'll have someone get started on searching road cameras too along this area. Maybe we'll get a hit on something."

"Thank you, Kent," Jake said, shaking his hand. "And thank you for sending Deputy Parkman to get me."

Kent glanced at Sabrina briefly then back at Jake. "I knew you would want to know. I also figured Sabrina would need you here with her."

She was glad she'd told Kent the truth about Jake and Robby. It would have been awkward to try to explain it in the midst of this chaos but now he understood why Jake had to be involved in this. Plus, he was right. She did need Jake with her now more than ever.

"You should go home," Kent suggested. "I'll let you know if there are any developments."

Jake nodded. "I'll take her home and stay with her."

Since Jake had no car with him and the car from the impound had two flat tires, Sabrina decided they could use her mom's car which was still sitting in the parking lot. Bob had taken her home and Sabrina still had the spare key. She climbed into the passenger seat as Jake eased into the driver's. She should have offered to drive given his injuries but she couldn't bring herself to do so.

They were nearly to her mom's house when she realized this wasn't where she needed to be. She'd followed along and let others decide for her, but she had to think of Robby. "I don't want to go home," she told him. "Turn around. Take me to the sheriff's office. I want to be there when something comes through."

"I don't think that's a good idea, Sabrina. Let your team do their jobs. I know you trust them."

Tears filled her eyes and she pushed back the wave threatening her. "Don't ask me to do nothing, Jake. I can't do that, not with Robby out there all alone. He needs me to find him."

He pulled to the curb at her mom's then reached out and took her hand and held it. "And we will. We'll find him. I promise. We'll bring him home where he belongs."

She was grateful to him for his support but her anguish was unbearable. She pulled her hand away as the truth of the situation hit her. He didn't want her there, he didn't want her at the station. He didn't want her involved and she needed to be involved. No one cared as much about bringing Robby home as she did and that included Jake.

He hadn't been in their lives because he'd left her the last time tragedy had struck.

She pulled her hand away from his as anger gripped her. She was tired of being told what to do. "You made me a lot of promises once, Jake, and you didn't follow through with them. How can I ever trust you now with something so important?"

"What are you talking about?"

"Years ago when my brother died, you swore to stand by me. Next thing I knew you were leaving town and not looking back."

"That's not fair, Sabrina. I tried to reach you."

"You proved to me and my son years ago that we couldn't trust you. What makes you think I can trust you now with my son's life. You already proved to me years ago that when the going gets tough, Jake Harris gets going."

She opened the car door and sprinted out and ran inside. She couldn't face him. And she certainly couldn't trust him to find her son.

She and Robby were on their own.

Jake watched her run into the house. He leaned back in his seat. His instinct was to go after her but nothing she'd said wasn't true. His face burned with shame at the way he'd left her years ago. He'd tried his best but now looking back he knew his best hadn't been good enough. He should have pushed to remain with her. He wouldn't make that mistake again. No amount of pushing him away to wallow in her grief was going to make him leave her, or Robby, ever again.

Still, it couldn't hurt to give her some space.

He turned the car around and headed back for the sheriff's office to check in on the investigation. Like her, he wanted to be there to see where the evidence led. He couldn't imagine what Sabrina was going through. He'd only known his son a short time but knowing Creed had taken him had left a gaping hole in his heart. He couldn't lose him now.

The department was bustling when he entered. It seemed everyone was on alert. He noticed Kent and Sheriff Thompson in the same conference room he'd been treated in earlier. It appeared to have been transformed into some kind of command center. He walked in and spotted Robby's photo, the one from the text message Sabrina had received, posted on a whiteboard along with details of the investigation.

Sheriff Thompson spotted him and walked over. "Agent Harris, it's good to see you up and moving better."

She extended her hand and he shook it. "Thank you. Is there any news?"

The sheriff glanced at the photo of Robby then shook her head. "Not yet. My team is still working on it. Is there a reason you're back here?"

She gave him a quizzical look and he realized she didn't know yet about his connection to Sabrina or Robby. "I just want to help if I can."

"I'm sure we have this under control," she assured him. She turned to Kent. "Keep me updated. I'll be in my office."

Jake approached Kent as the sheriff exited the conference room. "Sabrina said she'd told you the truth about me, Kent."

He nodded. "She did."

"But the sheriff doesn't know?"

He shook his head. "I've only known a few hours. I was trying to figure out the right way to tell her when I received the call about the abduction. I haven't told anyone."

Jake stared at the photo of Robby on the board. A swell of love and emotion for the child overwhelmed him. "I can't ever go back undercover in Creed's organization but we still need to preserve the investigation in case it ever goes to trial. I don't care who knows Robby is my son but I think for now we should limit the number of people who know I'm Jake and not Max."

"Agreed," Kent stated. "I spoke with Agent Price and he agrees too. However, I have to let Sheriff Thompson know but it won't go farther than that. No one wants to risk Creed going free on a technicality."

A deputy got up and placed a pin on a

map. "We've had another sighting," he stated.

Kent walked over to it and Jake followed him. "What is this?"

"We've been receiving tips all afternoon about the van used in the abduction. From the best we can piece together, it headed west out of town." He ran his finger down a line on the county map. Multiple pins indicated locations the van was seen.

"That's the wrong direction from where Creed's factory is located," Jake said.

"I noticed that too. It's possible like you said that he's taking Robby somewhere else to hold him or they could be circling around but that seems risky. The more mobile he is, the greater chance of being pulled over. So far, we lost them headed out of town but we've issued a BOLO to the neighboring towns and counties too. We're also issuing an Amber Alert for Robby. I used the photo that was sent to Sabrina's cell phone for the alert."

"Good thinking." He was glad to see Kent in action. It helped him to know that this office was capable of handling this situation. "We should still check out the factory."

"*We* will," he said, emphasizing the word *we* as a way of warning Jake to back off. "I've already told you I've got someone watching the factory. You should go back to the safe house. Creed is still targeting you."

Jake shook his head. "I'm more worried about finding Robby than I am about Creed coming after me."

"Then go be with Sabrina. She needs you now more than ever."

He was questioning that. "I'm not sure she does." She was strong, much stronger than he'd ever given her credit for. She'd pulled herself up from the dark pit of grief and depression, giving birth, and raised Robby alone for all these years. That was strength.

Kent leaned against the desk and locked

eyes with him. "She needs you now more than ever," he said again. "She's suffered enough. She doesn't need you letting her down again."

It was a strange thing for her boss to say. "Isn't that kind of personal."

"You're right that I'm taking this personally. She's part of my team and I care about Sabrina. I've watched her grow and learn and take on Creed's organization practically on her own. Then you showed up. She deserves better than to be left alone again."

"She practically told me to get lost," he argued but Kent wasn't letting him off the hook that easily.

"She's stubborn, that's for certain. And she lashes out when she shouldn't but it's just her defense. She needs you, Jake. She needs you to be there for her more than she's ever needed anyone at the moment. Don't let her down."

Jake realized Kent probably knew Sabrina better than he did. Or, at least, the woman she'd grown into since he'd left her. He was glad to know she had someone looking out for her. It was obvious to Jake that Kent was more than just Sabrina's supervisor, he was also a friend.

"You're right. She does. I'd better get back to her." As he headed back to the car, he realized Kent was right. He'd taken her refusal too personally. He was wounded too by Robby's abduction and trying too hard to make things right with her. He could never change the fact that he'd left her but he could prove to her that he would never do it again.

He drove back to the house. There wasn't much use watching his back as he drove but he still did. Creed wouldn't bother sending his men after them now. He had the upper hand and likely figured they would come to him when he called. And he was right. There was nothing he wouldn't do to get his child home safely. He made it to Beverly's house and parked. The lawn blow-ups were deflated and lying in a heap on the grass. It seemed to fit his mood. They shouldn't be up and happy without Robby around to see them.

He leaned against the steering wheel and did his best to catch his breath before getting out. He entered the house without knocking. Bev was in the kitchen sipping on a mug of something hot. Bob was by her side holding her hand. She still looked distraught and who could blame her. The photographs of Robby were prominently on display above the mantel, a reminder to everyone in the household who and what was missing.

He headed down the hall to the bedroom Sabrina had taken over but the door stood open and the room was unoccupied. When he turned, he spotted the playroom door standing open. He peeked inside and found her sitting on the floor surrounded by a sea of toys, a stuffed animal in her arms as she cried.

She looked up at him with anticipation in her face. "Is there any news?"

He hated to disappoint her. "Not yet but they're working on it. They've traced the van to the outskirts of town."

"Near Creed's factory?"

"No. The other way. Kent believes he's probably got Robby holed up in a hotel room somewhere. They're checking them all."

He slid down and sat beside her. This time, she didn't lash out when he put his arm around her. Instead, she leaned into his arms and sobbed, and Jake held her as she did.

Sabrina paced in front of the whiteboard in the conference room. She'd convinced Jake to bring her back to the sheriff's office but it hadn't been easy. They all wanted to treat her like some victim who needed to hide out in her bedroom. And she had, at least for a little while, but now she knew she had to be proactive if she hoped to find Robby. She couldn't allow Creed to win. She was going to get her son back.

She grabbed all the files she could on the men she'd associated with Creed. One of them had to be involved or know where he'd taken Robby. She pored through those files, picking out names to investigate. She'd arrested most of them at one time or another over the past several years so she knew them and their loyalty to Creed. It wouldn't be easy to break them but she had a new motive now.

She chose several names to bring in for questioning then went into Kent's office to share her findings.

He looked through her notes then sighed. "There's no way I'm giving you permission to go after these men."

"Why not? All of these men are known associates of Paul Creed. They need to be questioned about Robby's disappearance."

"None of these match the description of the man who abducted him from the park."

"But we didn't get a description of the driver."

"Look, I'll send people out to look for them and question them—"

"I should be the one to do it," she interrupted. This was her lead and, although she trusted her coworkers, she had more at stake and needed to ensure the proper questions were asked.

"There's no way I'm sending you out there. You shouldn't even be here. I told Jake to take you home, not back here. This is an open investigation that you don't need to be anywhere near."

She glared at him. "It's my son who's missing."

"Which is exactly why you can't be a part of the investigation. Your judgment is too clouded. I'll send the others to split up and find these men and question them. That'll have to be good enough."

She turned and stormed out of his office. It wasn't right that she was being shut out. She knew Creed and his men better than anyone else in this department.

The cell phone she'd tossed onto her desk dinged with a new message but Sabrina turned her head away instead of glancing at it. Robby's story was all over the TV news and police bands and had garnered so much attention that her phone had been blowing up for the last few hours. She was grateful for friends who cared but the constant bombardment of people who knew her sending her thoughts and prayers during this trying time was more than she could wrap her mind around. She didn't mean to be ungrateful because she was thankful to have people who cared about her, but she also didn't need the constant reminder that her son was missing. No one knew better than she and her aching arms that Robby was gone. Besides, Jana had set up a tracing alert on her cell in case someone other than her friends from her contacts tried to call.

All she wanted was her son back and she would do whatever it took to make it happen.

She glanced up and spotted Jake heading her way. He was still moving slowly but he was working through the pain to do what he could. He should have been resting but he was just as determined to find Robby and she appreciated that.

"How do you feel?" he asked as he slid into a chair beside her desk.

"How do you think?" She cringed at the sharpness of her tone. She didn't mean to take out her frustrations on him but she couldn't hold in her anger. She wanted her son back. "I'm sorry," she told him.

"You have nothing to be sorry about, Sabrina." He reached out and took her hand in his and she savored the feel of his strength. "I may not be moving so fast at the moment but I have strong shoulders. Feel free to place your burdens on them any time."

She squeezed his hand, grateful for the reassurance and that she wasn't alone in this.

"Have you called your mom?"

She let go of his hand and turned away. Her mom wasn't to blame for this and she knew her misplaced anger was irrational but she hadn't been able to bring herself to forgive her yet. She should have been watching Robby more closely. They both should have been. "No."

"You should. She's hurting, Sabrina."

"So am I." She blew out a frustrated breath. "I can't deal with her right now, Jake. I have to focus on getting him back. Once Robby is home then I can forgive her for not keeping him safe."

He nodded then leaned back in the chair, seeming to decide not to push the subject.

"Has there been any word?" she asked him. She knew he'd been talking with Commander Stover who headed up the patrol division. They'd established roadblocks in and out of town soon after the kidnapping at the park.

"So far there haven't been any further sightings of the van."

"So then they either got through the roadblocks before patrol set them up or else he's holding Robby somewhere inside the perimeter."

"Kent is checking all the motels in the area but there are dozens of places they could be holding him."

She knew that. "I made a list of known associates of Creed's and gave it to Kent. He's going to have the team go and question them."

"I think that's a good idea."

"I should be the one doing the questioning. I'm the one who knows these men." She was hoping he might back her up on that idea but instead he shook his head.

"It's better you let the others handle it. Those men all know you. You've questioned them before and they never gave up Creed. Maybe some new blood will change that. In the meantime, they've also got eyes on the factory."

She shook her head. She doubted he was there. Creed would make sure Robby was someplace where he wouldn't be found.

Her phone lit up and they both turned to look at it on the desk. She'd silenced it earlier but that hadn't stopped the messages and calls. She couldn't even bring herself to read the texts or listen to the voicemails. She switched it off then placed it inside a drawer. "I can't deal with people right now," she explained to him.

"I understand. Can I get you something? Anything? Coffee? Water?"

She shook her head as the tears threatened her again. "I just want Robby back."

"We're working on it. I promise you I'll bring him home, Sabrina. I promise." He stood then leaned over and kissed her. "I'm going to check in with Jana and see if she's had any headway with discovering if your mom's phone had been cloned."

Sabrina watched him go. She wanted to believe in him and his promises but she was scared to trust him again. She'd put all her hope and faith in him once only to be disappointed and let down. He'd left her when she'd needed him most. Now she and Robby both needed him.

She had to pull herself together if she had any hope of finding Robby. She couldn't allow Creed to win. She wasn't going to allow him to take someone else she loved from her.

After Jake left, she somehow found the strength to get up and walk to the restroom. She washed her face then stared at herself in the mirror. She had to be strong for Robby's sake. She loved him too much to fail him. She couldn't allow grief and despair to pull her under the way it had when her brother had died. She had to be stronger than that for her son's sake. She had to call on the strength he'd given her to do whatever she had to do to find him and bring him home.

"Lord, please bring my baby home."

That simple request sent waves of tears through her. Jake wasn't the only one who'd let her down. It felt like God had abandoned her years ago after her brother's overdose. Then Jake had left her and her father had died. She'd thought at the time that all that loss was more than she could handle. Only losing Robby was on a whole different level and, if God could bring her child back to her, she was willing to give Him a second chance.

She dried her face then walked back into the squad room only to find someone sitting beside her desk. Bob stood when he spotted her. "Do you have a moment to talk?"

She sighed. There was only one reason he would be here and she wasn't ready to face it. "I really can't—"

"I'm not here to scold you," he told her. "I just wanted to check in on the search for Robby."

"No, nothing concrete yet but my team is working on it and they're very competent." She might be struggling with trying to let go of control over the situation but she did trust the people she worked with to do a good job.

He nodded. "Good. I'll let your mother know."

Once he was gone, Sabrina walked into the conference room and stared long and hard at the whiteboard that contained all the evidence they'd collected so far about Robby's abduction. There had to be a clue in there somewhere that they were overlooking. There had to be something that indicated where Creed might be holding him.

A ding sounded and she gave a weary sigh. She'd thought she'd silenced her cell phone. She reached into her pocket to get it but it wasn't there. Only then did she remember she'd slipped her cell phone into a drawer.

That ding sounded again and she realized it was coming from her jacket pocket. She reached inside and pulled out a silver cell phone. It wasn't hers. In fact, she couldn't recall ever seeing it before.

She glanced around, wondering who could have slipped it into her pocket and when. The phone chirped again and she opened it. A message popped up with a photo—an image of Robby. His big blue eyes were full of tears and his face was scrunched with fear.

Tears filled her eyes as her heart raced and she quickly scanned the message.

Want to trade?

She gasped. He was willing to trade something for Robby's life.

Forgetting her concerns, she quickly texted back. Anything.

You for the kid. You come to me and I'll let him go.

She fell into a chair at the conference room table as the demand hit her. Creed wanted her to turn herself in to him. If she did, he would release Robby.

Her hands shook as she quickly responded. Deal.

Voices outside the door startled her, causing her to drop the phone. She quickly shoved it beneath the table with her foot as the door opened and Jake entered.

He put on a brave smile. "Hey, there you are. Kent is sending Deputies Shaw and Patterson to question the names on that list you gave him. He wanted to know if you had any particular questions you wanted them to ask or advice for them."

If Jake saw this phone and text message, he would want to confiscate the phone and try to use it to track Creed's movements. He would never allow her to trade herself for Robby, which was just what she was planning to do. "No, I trust them. They'll do fine."

He shot her a quizzical look. "Okay, if you're sure."

"I am. They're both excellent investigators. They'll uncover the truth. I just need a few minutes to myself, if that's okay."

"I understand." He hesitated by the door then turned back. "I'll be around if you need me."

As anxious as she was to get him out of the room so she could continue bargaining for her child's life, she suddenly realized he would never let her go. He would fight her tooth and nail. He wouldn't understand her need to do whatever she could do to get her son to safety. Plus, he was watching her like a hawk now. How was she going to get away to see Creed without him knowing? She couldn't. Jake would surely stop her before she could trade herself for Robby. Neither would anyone else in this department.

She had to get out of here and get rid of Jake.

Once he was out of sight, she leaned down and picked the silver phone back up. She quickly sent another text to Creed.

Where can we meet?

He sent back directions to meet at the shopping center, promising to release Robby there once she arrived. She was a little surprised that he hadn't told her to come to the factory. Of course, he probably knew the sheriff's office had it under surveillance by now.

On my way.

She slid the cell phone into her pocket then walked out of the conference room. Kent and Jake were huddled up talking to Drake and Lisa about questioning Creed's men and the others in the officer were occupied with their work. No one was paying her any attention.

Good.

She walked down the back hallway then slipped out of the station through the back door. Jake still had the keys to her mom's car but thankfully Sabrina knew she kept a spare in a magnetic case just above her tire. She quickly slipped it out then hopped into the vehicle and started it.

She pulled out of the parking lot of the sheriff's office and realized this would be her last time doing so. Tears filled her eyes at the idea of never seeing Jake again but she pushed those away. She couldn't concentrate on what she was losing, only on saving Robby's life. He would need Jake once she was gone.

She only hoped Jake could forgive her for what she was about to do.

She drove to the shopping area and parked away from other vehicles. She was about to text Creed to let him know she'd arrived when another car pulled up beside her and several men got out. She recognized one of them as Lucas Davis, the man who'd threatened her with a knife in this very parking lot.

She got out too, keeping her hands where they could see them. She didn't want any misunderstandings. "I'm unarmed," she said.

Lucas grabbed her then patted her down before nodding to another man in the car. He got out and opened the door to the back seat of the car. "Get in," he told her.

She hesitated, noticing the back seat was unoccupied. She backed away, suddenly having second thoughts about trusting Creed or his men. He'd assured her Robby would be there and he wasn't.

"Where's my son?"

"We're taking you to him. Now get into the car," the man demanded, his tone firmer this time.

Lucas shoved her and she bit back a retort. "He was supposed to be here. Creed promised he would release my son." Only now did it sink in to her how irrational she'd been to believe him and how foolish she'd been to leave without telling Jake.

She glanced around the parking lot. They were far enough away from the other cars that even if she screamed out for help, no one would reach her in time. Besides, she didn't see anyone anyway. Lucas grabbed her arm and, this time, shoved her toward the car.

She climbed into the back seat. Another man was sitting by the door and Lucas slid in on the other side of her. As the door closed and the car sped away, Sabrina knew she'd made a terrible mistake.

TEN

Jake slipped into the break room, pulled out some change then popped it into the vending machine for a drink. He had some over-the-counter pain relievers in his pocket and he took them out and swallowed several along with the drink. He didn't want to take anything stronger because he didn't want to be slowed down by them but, for now, he needed something to stem the rising pain he was experiencing.

He fell into a chair and rubbed a hand through his hair. He was doing his best to keep up a good facade for Sabrina's sake but it was difficult. Creed was dangerous and having his son in Creed's hands was overwhelming.

He took a deep breath then went in search of Sabrina. Her strength during this crisis amazed him. He'd been afraid that she would lose herself to grief and despair as she had when her brother died, but instead her determination had steadied her. It couldn't last, however. The longer he was gone, the harder it would be for her to maintain her tough demeanor.

Please, God, help us find him.

He checked her desk, and the photo of Robby as a baby stabbed a pain through his heart. It wasn't right. He'd only just found his son. He couldn't lose him now. And he didn't want to lose Sabrina either. No matter what happened, he wasn't letting this tear them apart. Nothing would separate them again.

He stuck his head into the conference room, surprised when she wasn't there. This was the last place he'd seen her.

"Have you seen Sabrina?" he asked of the deputies in the conference room.

They glanced at one another but all

282 Dangerous Christmas Investigation

shook their heads. "We haven't," one of them said.

He searched several more places, including knocking on the ladies' room door, before panic began to set in. He pulled out his cell phone to call her then remembered she'd turned her cell off and placed it into her drawer. He hurried back to her desk and opened it. Her phone was still there, still turned off. Her gun was in her drawer as well so at least he knew she hadn't gone anywhere.

At least, not anywhere officially.

Dread filled him. It wasn't like her to be out of contact, especially not today, not when she'd been so worried about missing news. He dialed her mother's number and wasn't surprised when Bob answered instead of Beverly.

"Is everything okay there?" Jake asked him.

"Sure, we're okay. I gave Beverly something to help her rest."

"That's a good idea. You haven't heard

from Sabrina, have you? I mean, she hasn't called, has she?"

"No, she hasn't. I know her mom would love to speak to her. She's so upset." Bob's tone changed as he must have been wondering why Jake would be asking. "Why? Has something happened?"

"I don't know yet. I'll call you back." He ended the call then hurried outside and burst through the back door, anger and fear settling into him as he noticed her mother's car was missing from the space where he'd parked it earlier.

What have you done, Sabrina?

Anger rolled through him at her recklessness. Why on earth would she up and leave this way without telling anyone where she was going? He didn't know but his gut told him it couldn't be good.

He hurried down the hallway and into Kent's office, hoping against hope that she was there but not at all surprised when she wasn't.

"What's the matter?" Kent asked, seeing his worried expression. "Is something wrong?"

Jake rubbed his face as the reality of the situation set in. "I can't find Sabrina. She's gone."

"What do you mean she's gone?"

"I can't find her anywhere and her car is missing. She's gone, Kent. She left."

Kent picked up the phone and typed in a number. Jake heard it ringing on the other end. "Her cell phone is still in her desk drawer along with her service weapon."

Kent hung up the phone. A worried expression crossed his brow. "Are we thinking that something happened to her?"

Jake didn't see how someone from Creed's organization could have gotten past all the deputies in the department in order to abduct Sabrina. She would have made that difficult for them. "I think it's more likely that she left on her own. She's going to face Creed."

Kent sighed and fell into his chair. "Why would she do that? That's suicide."

"We all know Creed is behind this. She must have decided to go and confront him herself. I should have been watching her more closely."

Kent picked up the phone again and hit a button. "Jana, I want you to scan Sabrina's emails and cell phone. I want to know if someone from Creed's organization managed to send her a message."

Jake hadn't considered that. "Good idea."

"I'm also issuing a BOLO for her and the car."

Jake was thankful for that. Hopefully, they could find Sabrina before she did something she couldn't come back from.

The car ride seemed to last forever but finally the car neared the factory. Lucas grabbed her head and shoved her down before they reached the factory gate, obviously so that whoever was watching, like the police, wouldn't see her. Someone opened the gate and the car pulled forward. Lucas released her and she glanced behind her and saw the gate being closed once they were through.

Panic gripped her. She'd been having second thoughts since the moment she'd climbed into the car trapped between two criminals. What had she been thinking? And why hadn't she told Jake what she was planning to do? Perhaps his talking her out of it wouldn't have been such a terrible thing.

The car stopped and the men got out of the car then held the door for her to exit. She reluctantly did, doing everything to remind herself that she was doing this for Robby. "I want to see my son," she demanded as she got out.

The men didn't respond except to lead her up the steps to the factory doorway. Once inside, she glanced around, expecting to see Paul Creed greet her. Instead, one of the men slid open a door then another shoved her inside. They grabbed her and tied her to a chair.

She struggled against them. "Where's Robby? Where's my son?" she cried.

"Mr. Creed will be in to speak with you later," one of the men stated as he tightened the ropes against her wrist.

They walked out, closing the door and leaving her alone. She had no idea what was going to happen or when. Creed had promised not to harm Robby. He was going to drop him at a shop and call the authorities. That was the deal they'd made for Sabrina turning herself in. Only, she had yet to see Creed since she'd given herself up.

She pushed back tears. She couldn't allow them now. She only prayed that he would keep his word and Robby would be safe. Hopefully, Jake would find him soon and she knew he would take care of him. That was one of the main reasons she hadn't told him about her plan. Robby needed at least one parent to bring him up. She wished she could be around to see it but she'd done what she had to do.

She was sad that she might never see Jake again and hated the way they'd left things. She'd pushed him away because she had to, not because she wanted to. She'd wanted to tell him how much she'd fallen for him again and that she wanted to have a future with him, but that hadn't been possible. He would have stayed with her and never allowed her to trade herself.

She was lost in her thoughts and worry and had no idea how long she'd been alone in the room before the door opened and Creed entered followed by two of his men.

She braced herself for whatever was about to happen. This couldn't be good.

Creed's grin was maniacal as he stood in front of her. "Hello, Deputy Reagan."

"Where's my son? Is he safe?"

"Don't worry about him. I gave my

word that I wouldn't harm him and I won't. My man is picking him up and bringing him here so you can see him and know that I kept my word. I'm a man of my word, unlike that friend of yours Max Harris, who infiltrated my organization and lied to my face every day."

He still didn't know Jake had fooled him. He didn't know the real Max was dead.

"What are you going to do with me?" She'd expected to be dead already but instead they'd tied her up and locked her in this room. And he was going to show Robby to her. What game was Creed playing?

"Oh, don't worry. We are going to kill you. However, my supplier has been putting so much pressure on me to get rid of you that I felt it only prudent to make sure he sees that you've been neutralized. He's on his way here now so you've got until he arrives and sees for himself to say your last goodbyes. I have to admit,

I won't miss your constantly badgering my employees and my operation."

"You won't get away with this," she told him. "The sheriff's office knows that if I go missing, they'll look at you."

"No. They might believe that at first but there won't be any proof. No one abducted you. You came willingly. We'll float the idea that you got Robby back then took off. You'll be missing and so will your vehicle. Don't worry. We'll set up some drops to make it look like you've been using your bank card along the way before you completely vanish."

"I would never leave my son. Anyone who knows me knows that."

He knelt beside her and smiled. "Of course you wouldn't. You and Robby are both going to disappear."

Her heart sank as she realized what he was saying. "You promised me that Robby would be safe. You gave me your word. You said you would drop him off somewhere safely."

"And I'll keep that promise. He is safe. I never agreed to return him to the sheriff's office. He'll be taken somewhere and given a new life. It's already been arranged."

She pulled at her binds and tried to lunge at him. "That wasn't our deal."

He jumped up and backward, then laughed at her futile attempt to get to him. "I'm changing the deal. Be thankful I'm letting you see him at all. He could already be on his way out of town to a new life with a new family."

He walked out the door and they locked her inside again. Only once he was gone did she let the sobs rock her. Robby was supposed to be safe. Creed had gone back on his word and now her son wouldn't be safe. Her attempt to trade herself for him had failed. Now she was going to die and her son would be left alone and vulnerable.

I'm so sorry, Jake.

She should have listened to him and

trusted him. If she had, they might all be safe and together.

Jake stared at a photograph of Sabrina and Robby sitting on the mantel at her mom's house and his heart clenched. *Why did you do it, Sabrina?* Why had she left them with no word at all? He turned away and to the current situation…telling Sabrina's mother what had happened to her daughter.

Beverly's chin quivered as she sat at her kitchen table with Bob, Jake and Kent and listened to Kent explain. "What do you mean she's missing too? Has that man done something to Sabrina too?"

Kent glanced his way and Jake intervened. "No, Beverly. We believe Sabrina left on her own to go confront Creed. We have video surveillance showing she got into your car and drove away on her own. No one was forcing her." He still couldn't believe how she'd slipped away. How he'd allowed her to slip away.

"But why?"

"To find Robby. She's certain Creed took him."

"And you don't know where she is? Why not go there and get her back?"

"We've been watching the factory where Creed set up shop but, so far, we've seen no sign of him or of Sabrina."

Beverly shook her head and Jake saw the despair shining in her face. He understood what she was going through. She'd already lost one child, now a grandchild and her daughter were missing too. "I knew this vendetta against Paul Creed was going to come to no good," she said.

Bob held her hand. "She's smart," he assured Beverly, then he looked Jake's way. "She wouldn't have gone off without a plan, would she? She must have had some idea where to find Creed or Robby."

Jake thought for a moment then agreed with him. "You're right. I think we would have found her by now if she wasn't.

Creed must have found a way to contact her."

"How?" Kent asked. "We've looked through her cell phone and her email. She didn't receive any messages and no department phone calls were routed to her."

"So maybe he contacted her in another way," Bob suggested. "Could it be someone inside your office that passed a message to her?"

Kent frowned and tapped his finger against the table nervously. That wasn't a prospect that any cop liked to think about. Finally, he had to concede it was possible. "I don't like the sound of that but I suppose it's feasible. Creed seems to have his hands in just about everything around town." He glanced at Jake, who saw something else brewing in that statement.

"Kent, has something happened?"

He nodded. "The warrants against Creed and the men who abducted you were denied by the judge. He wants more probable cause before he issues warrants. It might be nothing."

"Or Creed might have gotten to him. Having a judge in his pocket might explain how he's gotten away with his activities for this long."

"Sheriff Thompson is speaking with the DA's office but, for now, we can't arrest him. If he can do that, then he might have used someone in our office to reach Sabrina. I'll go back there now and start working on that angle. If he did contact her, we need to find out how and what he said."

Jake nodded. "I'm going to stake out the factory. I know it's a dead end but I have to do something."

Kent turned back to Beverly as he stood. "I'll call when there's news."

"Thank you, Kent." He turned to leave and Beverly called Jake. She stood and grabbed his arm. "Promise me that you'll find them, Jake. Promise me you'll bring them home."

He nodded then hugged her. "I will." Outside, he found Kent standing by the sidewalk waiting for him, a look of concern on his face.

"Jake, you shouldn't make promises to her that you can't guarantee to keep."

But Jake wasn't deterred. "I didn't," he assured Kent. "I will find Sabrina and Robby and I'll bring them both home." Nothing would stop him from putting his family back together.

Jake drove out to the industrial area of town but instead of heading to the factory, he planned to turn off earlier and meet up with the surveillance vehicle Kent had sent it to keep an eye on the factory after Robby's abduction at the park but, so far, the deputy on duty hadn't reported anything suspicious.

Jake wasn't sure what he planned on doing, but the answers to where Sabrina and Robby were had to be inside that factory.

His phone rang and he picked it up and glanced at the screen before answering. "Hey, Kent. Any news?"

"The car she was driving was found abandoned at the shopping center. Video cameras show her getting into another car with several men. We're working on identifying them and the car."

His heart sank into his stomach. Believing she'd gone to Creed was one thing but having it confirmed was another. "Did it look like she was being forced?"

Kent sighed. "They might have strong armed her into getting into the car, but she met up with them of her own free will. I've pulled employee records for the department and I'll start going through them. If we have someone in our office feeding Creed information, I want to know about it."

"Keep me updated," Jake told him and he promised to.

He didn't like the idea that Creed had eyes and ears in the sheriff's office but it didn't surprise him. Creed had to have gotten a message to Sabrina some way. He pulled into a clearing in the woods where another vehicle was parked. The deputy got out to meet him as Jake approached.

"Commander Morgan said you were coming by," the deputy, who Jake recognized as Deputy Parkman, explained.

Jake got out and shook the man's hand. "Have you seen anything?"

"There has been some activity, cars coming and going all day, but I haven't noticed anything that might indicate Deputy Reagan or her child is there."

He wasn't surprised. Creed was too smart to keep them in the one place Jake and the rest of the sheriff's department knew he operated out of. "I'm here to relieve you," Jake told the deputy. "Kent wants you to return to the station."

Deputy Parkman handed him a pair of binoculars. "I'll leave it to you."

He climbed back into his car and drove off. As he did, Jake used the binoculars to scan the factory. Much of it was hidden by the fence surrounding it but they were on a hill so they had a better angle. Plus, if he climbed onto the car, he got an even better view of the property. Some kind of activity was happening there. He spotted several trucks lined up along the outside loading docks and, as Deputy Parkman had stated, cars were continually coming and going.

He jotted down names of the men he recognized along with their activities. For the ones he didn't know, he wrote down descriptions. He even tried snapping pictures but they were just too far away to come out clearly.

He didn't really care about the drug activity at the moment. That was far down on the list of things he cared about, but it might be useful if it could help him in finding Sabrina and Robby.

He huddled in for the long haul. His phone was on vibrate in his pocket so he wouldn't miss a call. He'd never expected his heart could be so fragile until he'd learned he was a father and seen the glint in his child's face. He'd loved him from the first moment and everything in his life had changed in that instant. He'd gotten over his anger at Sabrina for keeping Robby's birth from him. It did nothing to help them move forward and he could understand the events that had led up to it. Again, if he hadn't left her, he would have known. Plus, he'd seen the dark place she'd been in after her brother's death.

Only, now he didn't know how he was supposed to live his life without his son, or Sabrina, a part of it.

A car turned off the main road and approached the factory. He watched as it stopped at the gate for entrance. He pulled out the binoculars and scanned it, seeing multiple people inside, including what looked like a car seat in the back surrounded by two men.

He jumped from the car and hurried closer through the brush for a better look before they disappeared through the gate. He lifted the binoculars and zoomed in. Dark hair was evident as the middle occupant in the car seat and, when one of the men turned to speak, he caught a glimpse of the child's face.

It was Robby.

His gut clenched as the car entered through the gate and it closed behind them. He slipped the binoculars' strap over his head then jumped up, grabbing ahold of a branch and climbing up into the tree for a bird's-eye view. He spotted the car when it stopped in front of the main entrance and the doors opened. Jake held his breath, praying he wasn't about to see what he thought he was about to see. Several men exited the vehicle then the little boy. The men each grabbed an arm and rushed him up the steps to the factory door.

He started to rise, clutching his gun then stopped. There was little he could do at the moment alone but, now that he knew Robby was here, he was determined to go in after him.

He pulled out his cell phone, ready to call Kent and update him on what was happening. He wasn't sure what their next move was but he wasn't leaving this place without his son. And he still needed to find Sabrina.

Before he could place the call, the doors opened again and Sabrina came out with Robby in her arms. She appeared to be sobbing softly and pressing Robby against her as she headed back to the car. She wasn't alone. The two men who had walked Robby inside were now following her, guns in hand, as she opened the back door of the car and strapped Robby back inside. Jake zoomed in on the vehicle as she kissed Robby's cheek then closed the door.

Jake held his breath and waited to see what was happening. What deal had she made to get Robby back and how could Creed allow her to just walk out?

Only she didn't get into the car. Instead, one of Creed's men climbed into the driver's seat. The other guy grabbed her arm and pulled her away from it.

She was letting this guy leave with Robby but she was staying behind. It made no sense to him. He couldn't believe what his eyes were seeing. Every instinct inside of him was telling him this was a mistake. It had to be a terrible mistake.

The goon grabbed her arm and pulled her back toward the doors as the car sped out of the parking lot with Robby inside.

Jake leaped from the tree, hightailing it back to his vehicle. He didn't understand what was happening but no deal where Robby was left alone with one of Creed's men was good. Whatever deal she'd made with him wouldn't be honored. She had to be aware of that.

He had to make a decision and fast.

He ran to his car and jumped in, starting it and pulling out. He knew where Sabrina was now but the farther away that car went, the less chance he had of finding Robby again. He now knew where she was but he couldn't help her at the moment.

He could, however, rescue his son.

Jake headed for the road, spotting the vehicle as it sped past him. He pulled out and followed the car. He didn't know where this guy was heading with Robby but he needed to intercept him. And, when he did, he would need backup to go back for Sabrina.

He pulled out his cell phone and dialed Kent, who answered right away. "Hey, what's up?"

"I just saw Sabrina trade herself for Robby."

"She did what?"

"They brought Robby to the factory. I watched her walk out and put Robby into a car with one of Creed's men."

"So she's been there this whole time?"

"I'm not sure. It's difficult to see past the gates but I definitely saw her buckle him into a car seat, then the car drive away without her. I'm following behind it now. I have no idea where he's going but this may be my one opportunity to get Robby back."

"Where are you?" Jake gave him directions. "I'm sending patrols and I'm right behind them. Don't do anything until we intercept you."

"Hurry," he said, unwilling to make any promises. He would rather wait on backup but if he thought for a moment that Robby's life was in danger, he would act. He wasn't going to risk losing Robby again. But he also had to be careful to make certain his son wasn't injured or taken captive again by the driver. His gut wanted to ram the car and run him off the road but that would only put Robby's life at risk even further.

"Just follow behind him without letting him see you," Kent instructed. "As long as he's driving, Robby should be fine. I've got cruisers on the way to you. We'll be discreet until we know where he's going and what he plans to do with Robby."

Jake agreed that was best. He was itching to get back to the factory and rescue Sabrina but she would want him to put Robby first so that's what he was going to do. Besides, he had eyes on his son. He didn't know what was happening with her at the moment.

He followed the car for several miles, doing his best to remain invisible. The driver didn't seem to notice he was being followed. He remained on the line with

Kent until the driver turned into a motel parking lot on the outskirts of town.

"He's at the Western View Inn. Looks like he's parking."

Jake parked too then got out and watched the scene unfold. He hid himself behind cars as he quietly approached them. Thankfully for him, the driver didn't get out right away or he wouldn't have had time to make it to him. He reached the side of the car and dared to peek through the passenger's side window. The driver was looking down at his cell phone while Robby was still in his car seat and appeared to be unharmed. Good.

The driver opened the door and got out and Jake saw the opportunity. He gripped his gun then popped up as the driver's side door closed but before he could open the back door. He trained his gun at the kidnapper. "Don't move," he told him.

The guy seemed startled and reached for the handle.

"I said don't move," he shouted and the man took a step backward and held up his hands.

Jake circled the back of the car, his gun still trained on him. "Now back away from the door."

The man did as he was told but his eyes were back and forth thinking of a way out of this. Suddenly, sheriff's office cruisers filled the parking lot. Two deputies hopped out and grabbed the man from behind, cuffing his hands.

"We've got him," Deputy Parkman assured Jake and only then did Jake relax and put his gun away.

He opened the back door, unbuckled Robby from his car seat. Red streaks lined his face, evidence he'd been crying. He sniffled and coughed as Jake released him then pulled him to him. Robby placed his head on Jake's shoulder and Jake rubbed his back.

"It's okay, Robby. You're safe now. No one is going to hurt you again."

He hurried him away from the car, not wanting Robby anywhere near even a single man of Creed's. An ambulance had arrived and parked on the outskirts of the scene so Jake headed there but, when he tried to hand him off to the waiting paramedic, Robby clung to him.

"No, don't leave me," he cried.

Jake's heart broke at the fear in his little boy's plea. He rubbed his hair and reassured him. "I'm not going anywhere, Robby. I'm right here with you."

He longed to be part of the activity going on at the motel but staying with Robby was more important at the moment. His son needed him and he wasn't moving until he calmed down.

He held Robby while the paramedic examined him. "He doesn't appear to have been harmed," he assured Jake. "Wherever they had him, they took care of him."

Jake breathed a sigh of relief. That was something at least.

Thank You, Lord, for bringing Robby back safely.

Kent appeared at the ambulance. "Has the suspect said anything?" Jake asked him. He could see the man he'd followed was now in the back seat of a patrol vehicle.

"His name is Allen Clifford. He has an extensive rap sheet for drug possession and robbery. He knows he's been caught red-handed in a kidnapping scheme so he's spilling everything. He was supposed to drop Robby off in room seventeen to a woman who was going to place him into foster care. He claims it's part of a scheme to get money from the foster care system for each kid."

Jake's stomach turned at the thought that, if he'd allowed this man to go through with his mission, his son might be lost to the system by another evil scheme of Creed's to make money.

"We're sending in a team now to the

hotel room to apprehend whoever is in there. How is Robby?"

"He's scared but he's not hurt. And he misses his mom."

Kent nodded. "We don't have the manpower to be in both places at once. We'll go take care of that once we're finished here."

Given his injuries, he'd already exceeded his physical limits and his body was refusing to comply with his desire to join in on the raid. Instead, he remained outside with Robby while Kent's team breached the room and took a woman inside into custody. He only hoped she hadn't been alerted to their presence and phoned Creed or someone else to warn them.

If they knew Robby had been rescued, they might have no reason to keep Sabrina alive.

Deputy Parkman approached the ambulance. "I can stay with Robby if you'd like," he offered. He reached out for

Robby and, to Jake's surprise, Robby reached out to him. "We're old friends, aren't we, Robby?" He shrugged at Jake's quizzical look. "Sabrina's brought him to the station a few times. If you'd like, I can make sure he gets back to his grandmother. I know Kent spoke with her and let her know he was safe."

Jake appreciated the offer but he hardly knew the deputy and he wasn't taking any further chances with Robby's safety. Only, he couldn't take him with him either and he needed to get back to Sabrina. He needed to trust someone in her department but given that there might be a mole working against them, his options were limited on that front.

"Thanks for the offer, Parkman, but let me talk to Kent about it first." Kent was really the only one in Sabrina's department that Jake trusted.

He waited until Kent returned from the raid then talked his options over with him. "I trust Parkman," Kent told him.

"But I'll go by and check in on him myself once we're done here if that will make you feel better."

"It would." That had to be good enough for Jake. Time was running out for Sabrina. He leaned down to Robby. "Deputy Parkman is going to take you to see Grandma, okay?"

Robby shook his head. "No. I want Momma."

"I know. You go get your grandma while I go get your momma." He reached out his hand to shake. "Deal?"

Robby giggled then shook his hand. "Deal."

Parkman ran and pulled the car seat from the car then buckled it into his cruiser before returning for Robby.

"Don't worry about him," Parkman said. "I'll make sure he gets home."

Jake handed him off and was glad to see Robby didn't fuss. "Your momma and I will see you soon," he promised

Robby. And he meant to keep that promise no matter what it took.

Once he knew Robby was safe, Jake turned back to the scene. He was just in time to see a middle-aged woman being led in cuffs to the back of a police cruiser. Jake bypassed her and headed to room seventeen. He glanced inside as Kent oversaw the room being processed.

He turned when he saw Jake. "Robby okay?"

"Yes. He wasn't harmed. Deputy Parkman is taking him back to Beverly's house."

"Parkman is a good guy. It's going to be okay."

He shot Kent a glare to remind him of what he knew about his suspicions that someone in the department was working for Creed. "What's happening here?"

"The woman we just arrested is named Gilda Mitchell. She's a state social worker from Alabama. Apparently, the plan was that she would take Robby and claim he was found abandoned. In return, she gets a kickback for placing him into the foster care system and he's placed with a family more interested in making money than caring for kids."

It was the worst part of the system. People always tried to game it and his son was nearly a pawn in it.

"How did Creed get involved in that scheme?"

Kent shrugged. "Too early to say. I'm sure he knows people involved. The organization pays him for the child and he's rid of him without actually having to harm him. Paul Creed is definitely a bad guy but it takes a certain kind of evil to directly harm a child."

"Did his man have any information about Sabrina?"

"Not much. He's only a driver. Apparently, Creed promised to let her see Robby so they took him to the factory for that meet-up."

Jake rubbed his face as the evil of the

world rattled him but he did his best to shake it off. He had to because he still had one more person he loved to rescue. He was ready to get Creed and his men out of the world for evil deeds and in jail. And he was ready to go find Sabrina and bring his family back together once and for all.

ELEVEN

Jake paced in front of the cars at the motel. He needed to get back to Sabrina before something terrible happened to her. Every moment he wasn't there, her life was in danger.

"Calm down," Kent barked at him. "You can't go in alone. You could place both your lives at risk."

"I can't keep standing here and doing nothing either," Jake told him. "Now that I know Robby is safe, I need to go find his mother."

He couldn't allow himself to think about the danger she was in. They'd discovered the plan for Robby but he doubted Sabrina's life would be spared. Creed had made it clear that he and his supplier wanted her dead and out of their way. He glanced at his watch and realized he'd already been gone for so long.

He couldn't wait any longer. "I'm outta here."

"Where do you think you're going?" Kent demanded as he walked off.

"You know where. I can't let anything happen to her."

"You can't go, not without a plan of action. We only have a small tactical team and they're regrouping after breaching the hotel. We need to finish up here first."

Kent and his team were still processing the hotel scene and he knew how long it took for forensics teams to finish. He couldn't wait. "It might be too late by then. I'm sorry, I have to go."

"I can't let you do this, Jake."

He stopped at his car door and looked back at him. Kent didn't seem to understand that nothing was going to stop him. "You can't really stop me. I don't work for you, Kent. I'm going to find Sabrina and bring her home no matter what you say."

He climbed into his car and took off before they could argue any longer. He didn't have to wait for the sheriff's office to come up with a plan. He needed to put eyes on her, needed to reach out to her and tell her how much he loved her. He couldn't risk waiting any longer.

He knew waiting would be prudent. They needed a plan to breach the factory and the sheriff's office could come up with that once but Jake was going in first, alone, to find her. His gut was telling him there was no time to wait. It had already been over an hour since she'd traded herself for Robby.

Time was not on their side.

He pulled off the road before he reached the factory and parked in the same clearing he had earlier. He got out, checked his weapon, then moved through the brush and grass until he spotted the factory. He took out his binoculars and scanned the area for the best place to enter covertly, picking out a portion of the fence he could climb over without being seen. Once over, he could hide in the brush, then make his way along the side of the building to the door. It was his best chance of sneaking in unseen.

Headlights approached and Jake crouched down. He took out his binoculars and watched as a car approached then stopped in front of the factory. The doors opened and two of Creed's men Jake didn't know by name stepped out, only they didn't appear alarmed by this car. It must hold someone they were expecting.

Jake jogged down the embankment to the fence and readied himself to climb over it once these men went back inside. He didn't want to risk getting captured before he could enact his plan to get inside and find Sabrina.

The engine shut off and a man got out

of the car. He glanced around the lot then headed into the factory.

Jake zeroed in on his face then stumbled backward in shock as he recognized the man.

What was he doing at Creed's organization and why were Creed's men not questioning his presence?

He moved up the steps and was led inside. Creed's men didn't even have their guns drawn as they escorted him into the building.

They slammed the door behind him and Jake pulled out his cell phone. He was still going in after Sabrina, but the sheriff's office needed to be alerted in case they didn't make it out.

Kent answered immediately. "Jake, please tell me you've changed your mind. I can have a team to the factory in less than an hour."

"I can't do that," Jake replied. "I'm going in after Sabrina but I thought you'd like to know I figured out who has been leaking information to Creed."

Sabrina wiped tears from her eyes as she huddled against the wall. Her hands were still tied but they hadn't rebound her feet after they'd let her see Robby. Creed had at least honored that. Only placing her child into that car and watching someone else drive away with him had broken her. She didn't know what was going to happen to Robby but she prayed he would be safe.

God, please keep him safe. Don't hold my foolishness against him. She was sorry she'd been so stubborn and angry at God. She understood now that her anger had been misdirected. She should have allowed God, and the people in her life, to comfort her in her times of grief, not push them away. That hadn't solved anything for her. In fact, it had only created more problems.

"I'm sorry," she cried out. The idea

that she was going to give God one more chance to prove Himself to her was laughable to her now and proof at how far she'd distanced herself from Him. He didn't owe her another chance, but she prayed He would give it to her and knew He would.

She was in this mess because she hadn't trusted God or the people in her life. She'd targeted Creed out of revenge and pettiness over her brother's death. She'd set herself on a mission and now her child was lost because of it.

God had brought Jake back into her life at least so Robby had one parent out there searching for him.

Find him, Jake. Please find our baby boy!

If only she had trusted him instead of having to do everything on her own. That no longer mattered and she hoped Jake would know that if it came down to a choice between saving her or Robby that she hoped he would choose Robby.

She had to trust now that he wouldn't stop until he brought Robby home. She knew that. She took a deep breath then released it as a sob as she realized the truth—she'd fallen in love with Jake again. She wished she'd told him that before she'd left. Now he might never understand why she'd done what she'd done or that she'd longed for a future with him.

The door opened and Sabrina wiped her face on her sleeve as Creed walked inside. He wasn't alone either. This time, in addition to his men, he had a visitor with him. She couldn't see his face immediately but she recognized he was different from the other men she'd seen before from his gray hair. Must be his supplier come to make certain she was taken care of once and for all.

"And this is Deputy Sabrina Reagan, the deputy who has been harassing my men and interfering with our operation.

Now that we have her, she won't give us any more hassles."

She didn't look up at the men who meant to do her evil. She didn't need to look them in the face knowing what they planned to do with her.

"I'm familiar with Deputy Reagan," the man stated.

Sabrina's heart stopped as she recognized that voice. She looked up, stunned at the face that stared back at her. She knew Creed's supplier well…and so did her mother. Creed's supplier, the man who wanted her dead, was Bob Crawford, her mother's boyfriend.

Confusion washed over her at the recognition. "Bob? What—what are you doing here?"

She couldn't wrap her head around it. He'd always been so nice to her but all the while he'd been running drugs and having Creed do his legwork? He was the man behind Paul Creed's operation? She felt ill thinking about how gentle and caring he'd been with Robby. How could she have let this monster around her son?

"It's nice to see you again, Sabrina."

Anger exploded inside of her. He'd been in her house, around her mother and son. He'd pretended to be a decent human being. She couldn't find the words so she simply lunged at him.

They all jumped back before Bob laughed. "Now, now, don't take this so personally."

Suddenly, her voice returned. "Don't take this personally? You've been dating my mother, you're trying to murder me and you've sent my son off somewhere. How can I not take that personally?"

"You've made your own bed, Sabrina. If you hadn't kept coming after these men transporting my product, your family would have been fine."

Anger burned her cheeks. "My brother wasn't fine after using your product."

He knew all about her brother, Robby, and how his death had affected them all yet he was still trying to feign innocence and place the blame on her. "If he hadn't died, maybe I wouldn't have been coming after your organization so intently."

She didn't see an ounce of empathy or regret in his expression. "Your brother made his own choices. You can't blame me for that."

"I can and do. I blame you all."

"Don't worry about your mother. She'll be understandably upset about your disappearance but I'll be there to make sure she's taken care of…and to, of course, reinforce a reasonable explanation about how you took off with Robby. I'm thinking that perhaps your agent Harris—Jake—broke your heart again and you couldn't bear it so you packed up Robby and left town. She'll turn to me for comfort and I'll be there for her." He knelt in front of her. "I want you to believe me when I say this, Sabrina. I truly do care for your mother."

Sabrina pulled at her binds again and

tried to lunge. "Stay away from her. You're a monster."

He laughed then stood and turned to Creed. "Go ahead and have your men take care of her, but do it outside of town. I have a truck heading out on a long haul. Place her inside it and they can dump her body once they're out of the state."

"Will do," Creed said.

Bob turned back to Sabrina and she glared at him again. "How can you look my mother in the face and pretend to care what happened to her family?"

"I care deeply about your mother, Sabrina. I didn't want this. This was all your doing."

"Jake will never give up looking for us. Never."

He looked confused then seemed to understand. "Why not? From what I hear, he's already left you once when you pushed him away. He'll do so again or else he'll pay the price too. Nobody gets in the way of my business." He turned to Creed and his voice hardened. "Clean this up or else. Then, we'll do business."

He sounded like a different person and she suspected that was his normal tone. He put on a face while he was with them but this was his real persona—a drug-dealing murderer. And her mom wouldn't know the difference until it was too late.

"I always knew there was something about you that I didn't like," Sabrina told him as he was walking out.

Bob turned to her one last time, smiling. "Shame on you, Deputy, for not trusting your instincts."

Crawford walked out and Creed turned to his men. "Grab her and take her outside. Let's end this once and for all."

His men came over and grabbed her arms, pulling her to a stand. She dug in her heels and went limp. "I won't go. You can't do this," she cried.

Creed stomped over and smacked her hard. Pain seared through her and the men lost their grips as she crumpled to the floor.

She clutched her cheek and glared up at him, her face stinging from the hit. She wouldn't let him see her fall apart. She might die, but he wouldn't get the added bonus of seeing her beg for her life.

"Get her," Creed told his men who grabbed her again and pulled her up. "Toss her into the trunk of the car while I go find out where this truck is located. I'll text you the information."

One of the men grabbed her from behind and held her while the other gagged her so she couldn't scream for help. It didn't matter. Who would hear her all the way out here? No one was coming to help her. She was on her own.

They dragged her to the doors then down the steps toward the parking lot.

The one with the keys hit the key fob and the trunk popped open on a car parked a few feet away. This was it. They were going to place her into that trunk

then kill her and dump her body somewhere out of state.

Bob Crawford would get away with
murdering her, all the while pretending
to care for her mother.

She'd failed Jake and Robby and now
she'd failed her mom too.

Jake crouched beneath a set of steps
as the factory door opened and two men
walked out, shoving Sabrina in front of
them. He recognized them as Dax and
Ethan, the same guys who would have
killed him if he hadn't gotten away from
them. He gripped his gun and assessed
the situation. Sabrina's cheek was red
and she looked to have been crying and
that angered him. If they'd harmed her,
they would have to answer to him.

He scanned the area. The parking lot
was clear of people. Everyone else, including Creed's newly discovered partner, Bob Crawford, must still be inside.
He hadn't noticed them exiting the build-

ing. Of course, if he was involved then he must be overseeing the operation.

Ethan and Dax pushed Sabrina toward a waiting car and opened the trunk. He couldn't wait any longer to act. Once they had her inside, they would kill her… just as they'd planned to do with him.

He was too far away from his own vehicle to get to it in time to catch up with them and follow them. He wished he were. He would much rather take the risk of running them off the road than having to confront them at such a central location. Creed and his other men could emerge from the factory at any moment.

He had no choice. He had to act now.

Sabrina looked terrified as Dax grabbed her arm and pulled her toward the open trunk. She jerked away from him but he pulled her back and shoved her down. Jake acted while they were watching her and darted toward the car. He slammed the butt of his gun against Ethan's head. Dax spotted him and slammed the trunk, reaching for his gun as Ethan collapsed on the asphalt.

"I wouldn't," Jake told him as he reached for his gun.

Dax reluctantly moved his hand away and held it up. He stole a glance at the factory and, for a moment, Jake worried someone might be behind him. He changed positions so that he could see both the factory entrance and the man.

Jake reached in and grabbed Dax's gun from its holster. "Get on the ground," he instructed and Dax did as he was told. Jake searched him for the keys and found them. He popped open the trunk, barely missing a kick from Sabrina as he did.

She gasped when she saw him and took his arm, quickly climbing out. Jake cut her hands free and removed the gag then pulled her to him.

"You came for me," she gasped.

"Of course I did. I wasn't going to let Creed hurt you."

"Robby! They took Robby."

He touched her cheek to calm her. "He's fine. He's with your mother."

"But how?"

"I was here when you loaded him into that car. I followed it to a motel where they were going to hand him off to a social worker from out of state. I got him out."

She nearly collapsed in his arms with relief. Tears slid down her cheeks. "Thank you for making sure he's okay."

"I would never let anything happen to him. I promised you that."

She nodded. "You did."

He leaned his forehead against hers, so overwhelmed by the feeling that she was with him. They still needed to get away from these men but, at the moment, he was thankful she was alive. "How could you trade yourself to Creed like that? How could you do it?"

"I had to do something to protect Robby. I didn't want anything to happen to him."

"You had to know Creed wouldn't keep his end of the bargain."

Her eyes widened. "It wasn't Creed who put the hit on me, Jake. It was Bob Crawford. He's been spending all this time with my mom at her house and he ordered me to be killed and Robby to be taken away. He's the supplier behind Creed."

He nodded. "I know. I saw him when he walked into the factory. I could hardly believe my own eyes."

"I never suspected him, not once."

"He'll get what's coming to him but, first, we need to get out of here."

He spotted a pack of zip ties in the back of the trunk and used them to bind Dax's hands then forced him into the trunk. As he slammed it, he handed the gun to Sabrina then pushed her toward the gate where he'd climbed over.

"Let's get out of here before someone else comes out." He took a moment to send Kent a message letting him know he'd found Sabrina. Kent had promised his team would arrive in an hour and it had already been over thirty minutes. "Reinforcements should be on the way."

They darted across the parking lot and reached the gate. Jake interlocked his hands together and she placed her foot into them, lifting her to the top. She quickly climbed over.

He heard commotion and turned to see a man descending the factory steps and running to Ethan, who was still on the ground unconscious. He called for help and Jake knew their time was limited before they were discovered.

He scrambled up the fence but not in time. The man spotted him and called out. "Hey, you! Stop!"

Jake hit the ground on the other side and, by the time he did, several more men he didn't recognize were exiting the building. He spotted both Creed and Bob and knew they'd been discovered.

"Let's go," he said, pushing Sabrina to

run up the embankment to where his car was parked.

She hurried up the hill and he was right behind her, pushing her to go faster.

It wasn't fast enough. Several shots rang out and hit the tree as he ran by. He stopped and crouched behind it. They'd already gotten weapons that could reach at this distance. He spotted someone with a rifle. He might be able to shoot this far but his aim wouldn't be good. He also spotted armed men heading for the fence and climbing over. They were coming after them.

"How far is your car?" Sabrina asked.

"That way," he said. "It's not too far. We can hide in the trees. They've only got one rifle and his aim won't be good at this distance."

He urged her on and the shooter fired as they moved. He kept going. Stopping wasn't an option. They had to get to his car.

They made a dash through the clearing and spotted his car. His heart leaped at the sight.

Sabrina swung open the door and climbed inside while Jake followed. He turned the key then backed up and turned around before speeding away.

"We did it," Sabrina said giving a relieved laugh. She leaned over and hugged him. "You saved me."

He was about to congratulate himself when shots rang out and one whizzed past her face and through the windshield, cracking it.

Sabrina screamed and another shot rang out, sending the car out of control. Jake fought to keep it on the dirt path but another bullet nipped at his shoulder and the pain was blinding.

"Jake, watch out," Sabrina screamed just before the car went off the path and rammed into a tree.

They were both thrown and Jake slammed into the steering wheel. Pain doubled him over and the gun slipped from his hand.

He did his best to catch his breath and get his bearings but his breath caught when he spotted Sabrina on the floorboard. There was blood on her head and she was unconscious.

Movement in the rearview mirror told him Creed's men were closing in. He leaned over to try to retrieve his weapon but it was just out of reach and all the blood seemed to rush to his head. He struggled to move as darkness played at his vision.

If he lost consciousness now, they were both dead, but he couldn't stop the darkness that pulled him under.

TWELVE

Sabrina groaned as the pain in her head brought her back to consciousness. Everything hurt to move but she had to, the memory of the attack flooding back to her. She opened her eyes and saw Jake slumped over the steering wheel. A splotch of blood was on his shirt at the shoulder indicating he'd been shot.

She reached for his hand and felt for a pulse. He was still breathing. *Thank You, Jesus.* He was still alive.

Movement outside the car told her it wouldn't be for long. Creed's men were out there while she and Jake were trapped inside this vehicle. She'd seen the front end smash against the tree and, even now, could hear hissing as the engine's fluids released. They weren't going anywhere in the car.

She felt in her pocket for the gun Jake had handed her but it wasn't there. She searched the floorboard but couldn't find it but she spotted Jake's gun under his leg. She reached over and grabbed it as footsteps neared the car. They were coming.

From her position, she could see each window and saw when two figures approached the car, one on each side. She saw they each were armed. She didn't even wait for them to reach for the door. She fired through the window, hitting the one on her side of the car then the other. She heard them both hit the ground and scrambled off the floor. She peeked through the window. They were both on the ground. She opened the passenger door and got out and ran to the one on the ground beside her side of the car. She kicked away his gun then checked for a pulse. He was dead. She cautiously ran to the other and didn't even have to check him for a pulse. It was obvious from the hole in his head that he wasn't getting back up. She was a good shot.

She opened the driver's door and tapped Jake's cheek. "Wake up," she told him. "Wake up. We have to get out of here."

As she'd suspected, the car's front end was a mess. They weren't driving out of here in this car, which meant they needed to get somewhere to hide before the rest of Creed's men arrived.

Killing two of his men wouldn't help to endear her to him.

She tapped his cheek again and he finally roused. "Wake up, Jake."

He groaned. "What happened?"

"We wrecked the car. Come on. We have to get out of here."

She pulled him from the seat and he struggled for a moment to steady his legs.

"Can you walk?"

"Give me a second," he responded.

She heard voices floating on the air. "I'm not sure we have seconds."

She grabbed him under his arm to help steady him then led him away from the car and into the brush. They were moving slowly but at least they were moving. Creed's men would start searching for them once they discovered the car.

Sabrina couldn't get her bearings. She'd been in these woods many times but she was turned around either out of fear or from the crash. Her ears were ringing and she felt a little dizzy but she wouldn't let that stop her. They had to keep moving if they were going to survive this.

And they had to survive for their son's sake.

Jake steadied as they walked and soon they were dashing. She spotted the roof of something that looked like a building through the brush. "I need to stop here

344   *Dangerous Christmas Investigation*

for a minute." She leaned him against a tree then walked to the brush.

She spotted the old sawmill and realized where they were. They could take refuge inside there until they could figure out a way to find help and make certain that Jake's shoulder wound wasn't life-threatening.

She walked back to him. "We're near the old sawmill. We can take shelter there for a few minutes."

He leaned on her as they made their way through the brush to a dry creek where they crossed over. She pushed open the door and went inside then helped Jake to sit down. On the other side of the room, she spotted a chair and ropes on the ground.

"What do you think that's from?"

He grimaced. "That was for me. This is where Jacoby and his men held me after we left the high school."

He unbuttoned his overshirt then took it off and pulled up the sleeve of his

T-shirt so she could examine his wound. The bullet had only grazed him but it was bleeding heavily and running from Creed's men wasn't helping that.

"Here, use this as a bandage," he said, holding out his top shirt.

She took it from him and tore it into several pieces she could use to bandage his shoulder and stop the bleeding.

"We have to find a way to call for help," she told him and Jake agreed.

He dug through his pockets then groaned. "My cell phone must have fallen out of my pocket when I was climbing over the fence. If we can make our way to the highway maybe we can flag down a car. That's what I did when I escaped from Jacoby's men."

"Then that's what we'll have to do."

"Kent knows I'm here. He promised to send backup so help is at least on the way."

That was good news. So they just had to survive until the cavalry arrived.

"They'll be looking at the factory for us so it might take them some time to figure out what happened."

He shook his head. "Parkman knows about the clearing where I parked. Hopefully, he'll check it out and see the car. They'll know we're running through the woods."

She hoped they made it in time but, in case they didn't…

She leaned in and kissed him. He was startled at first but then he relaxed and kissed her back. "I love you, Jake."

He stroked her cheek. "I love you too, but don't give up on us yet."

"I'm not but I wanted you to know. When I thought I was going to die, all I could think about, besides Robby, was you and the fact that I never told you how much you mean to me."

He shook his head. "Why did you do it, Sabrina? Why did you give yourself to Creed?"

"I did what I thought was right to save Robby."

"Did you really think Creed was good for his word?"

She shook her head, feeling her face warming with shame. "I wasn't thinking. All I knew was that I couldn't lose him. Are you certain he's safe?"

He nodded and held her close. "I promised him I would bring you home. I plan on keeping that promise."

He kissed her and she sank into his arms. This was something she thought she might never experience again and she wanted it to last. She wanted a future with Jake. Five years ago, she hadn't been able to look past her own pain and grief to see how life could be good again but now she knew, with him and with God's guidance, they could be a family.

Suddenly the doors swung open and they were surrounded. Sabrina grabbed the gun she'd dropped on the ground then scrambled to her feet with Jake behind her. She didn't aim it at them as Creed, Bob and two other men had them cornered. Instead, she tucked it into her back waistband out of sight.

Creed grinned at them. "You thought you could come in and take her?" he asked Jake. "You thought wrong. Neither of you will get away with this."

"The sheriff's office is on their way here now," Sabrina told him. "Leave now before you're arrested."

Bob laughed. "The cops are busy out looking for Robby. Trust me, Creed. They're preoccupied."

"Is that what you think?" Jake asked him. "They're not looking for Robby any longer. He's safe and sound back at Beverly's house."

Bob scoffed. "That's not true."

"We found your man, Allen Clifford, Creed, heading to the Western View Inn to hand him over to that lady from out of state." He squeezed Sabrina's shoulders.

"Robby is safe and you'll never get your hands on him again."

Bob pulled out his cell phone, pressed a button then placed the phone to his ear. The tension in the air was palpable as he tried to verify Jake's story. Sabrina felt the tension in Jake and said a silent prayer that what Jake had told her was true, that Robby was safe. She knew he wouldn't lie to her but she also needed reassurance that her child was no longer in danger.

She shot arrows at Bob. He'd sneaked into their lives and, for whatever reason, had become enthralled with them. Had his plan all along been to keep eyes on her or had he actually cared for her mother as he'd told her?

She glanced at Bob and saw his face pale. He ended the call then threw his phone against the wall.

Creed stepped toward him. "Then it's true?"

Bob nodded. "They have your man in

custody along with the social worker. And, yes, the boy is back with his grandmother. I just spoke with her."

Sabrina's heart leaped with joy. She'd trusted Jake's word but to hear it confirmed was elation. Robby was safe. Even if she and Jake didn't make it through this, at least he would be okay.

Suddenly, she felt something at her back and realized Jake was going for the gun. She stiffened as he did, realizing he meant to fight them. She wasn't against fighting back but one gun wasn't going to get them out of this mess.

While Creed was focused on Bob, Jake pulled his gun and stepped in front of Sabrina. He held it against Creed's head.

Suddenly, everyone's attention was on them.

Creed laughed. "You're not going to kill me, Jake."

"You threatened and harassed the woman I love and you abducted my son to use as a distraction while you tried to kill his mother. I don't think I'll have a difficult time killing you, Creed."

"Max would never have—"

"Max couldn't stand you, Creed. He wanted nothing more than to bring you down. He despised every moment he spent with you. Besides, I'm not him. He might not have killed you but he might have if he'd lived through what I have these past few days."

He grabbed Creed's arm then backed up toward the door. "Now, we're going to walk out of here and no one is going to come after us or this is going to end badly for your leader here," he warned them all.

Sabrina ran to the door and opened it while Jake led Creed out, keeping the gun trained on him. The others were watching them closely, ready to strike but they didn't move, obviously waiting to see what happened.

She hurried through the door with Jake behind her. Only, seconds after she stepped through, another of Creed's men who'd remained outside grabbed her and clamped his hand over her mouth.

Sabrina tried to scream and Jake heard her. He spun around, the gun pulling away from Creed, who took advantage of the situation and tried to grab it from his hand. The others raced from the building, another one of them running over and helping restrain her. They dragged her away as Jake and Creed struggled for the gun. She was helpless to intervene and Bob didn't seem to care enough to do so.

As the men held her, he approached her, his usually kind face morphed into a snarl. He was angry that his plan had been disrupted and she couldn't help herself. She smiled at his discontent. To know that Jake had thwarted his plans gave her a moment of satisfaction.

"I've spent years building up my business, Sabrina, and I'm not going to let you and a fake undercover agent show up and ruin it."

"When did you know about Jake?" she asked him. "Did my mother tell you?"

"Not right away. She kept that secret until after Robby had been taken. By then, Creed already knew his friend Max was a cop. It didn't matter what his name was."

She stole a glance at Jake, who was still struggling with the gun. "Aren't you going to stop them?"

He shrugged. "I'll let Creed deal with him while I deal with you." He threw back his hand then punched her, sending her to the ground. Pain radiated through her and she was temporarily stunned, unable to move through the pain.

Suddenly, a cry rang out. She startled and looked over to where Jake and Creed were huddled together still fighting for control. Jake fell holding his leg and she saw blood pooling around his fingers and a knife protruding from his thigh.

Creed laughed but Jake quickly used his other leg to sweep over Creed, sending him to the ground. They both scrambled for the gun that had fallen. Jake reached it first and fired. Creed crumpled to the ground.

That was enough for Bob. He grabbed Sabrina by the hair and pulled her up. "I'll kill her," he said, but he'd hardly gotten the words out when lights and sirens lit up the area and multiple Mercy County Sheriff's Office SUVs surrounded them.

Bob tossed her to the ground then took off running with several deputies taking off after him.

Sabrina jumped to her feet and ran to where Jake was lying on the ground. She pressed her hand against his leg. The shoulder wound hadn't been bad but this one looked worse.

"We need help," she cried and Kent hurried over.

"Call for an ambulance," he shouted. "We have a man down."

"I'm okay," Jake said, trying to sit up. "I don't think it's very deep." He touched Sabrina's face and she leaned into his hands as tears welled up in her eyes. "It's over," he told her. "It's over and we're safe."

She kissed him and was so thankful that he'd come for her. "What about Bob?" she asked Kent.

"My men will catch him. He can't get far. There's already a warrant out for his arrest. We issued it after Jake alerted us he was there along with ones for Creed and his men. The judge finally came through. Turns out he was just being overly cautious. I have a team readying to search Bob's house and business."

"Trucking might have been his legitimate business, but he used it to transport drugs," Jake said.

"My mother will be heartbroken. She thought he truly loved her."

Jake held her hand. "Your mom is

strong. She'll be happy to have you and Robby back with her."

"What about Creed?" Sabrina asked then realized she knew the answer as she spotted him lifeless several feet away. He was dead. He couldn't harm her, or anyone, ever again.

Jake was right. This nightmare was truly over.

Sabrina watched as her mom pulled another tray of Christmas cookies from the oven and placed them on the table to cool. She was putting on a good face for Robby's sake and he was having a good time helping her decorate cookies for Santa, but Sabrina knew her heart was broken over Bob and his involvement with Creed.

They both turned as the small kitchen TV showed news footage of Bob, along with Mick Jacoby, Ethan, Dax and many others from the organization, being arrested by the sheriff's office and led away in handcuffs two days prior. Her mother's face paled at the reminder and she quickly picked up the remote and clicked off the television. The arrests were all over the news and Creed's organization, as well as Bob's trucking business, had been dismantled once and for all. Drugs may still find their way into Mercy County but, if justice prevailed in these cases, these men wouldn't profit from it. And the cases against them seemed strong. Jana had finally been able to decrypt that flash drive Jake had stolen, which linked Bob to Creed's organization. That was more evidence the DEA could use to dismantle his operation and flush out his connections to other drug organizations.

Sabrina put her hand on her mom's arm. "Are you sure you're up for this?"

She nodded and patted Sabrina's hand. "I need to stay busy."

"Whenever you're ready to talk about it, I'm here," she said and her mom hugged her, then quickly composed herself and turned back to the cookies, picking up a tin of icing. "Robby and I are going to decorate cookies then make some hot chocolate and watch a Christmas cartoon, aren't we, Robby?"

He cheered and licked the spoon for the icing.

Sabrina was happy to see him settling back so well after all he'd been through. She kissed the top of his head and rubbed his hair. She'd nearly lost him and had worried about residual effects but, so far, he seemed fine. They hadn't harmed him and, for that, she was thankful.

"I'll be in the garage putting the you-know-what together," she whispered to her mom, who gave her a conspiratorial wink.

She walked outside to her mom's car and opened the trunk where earlier in the day she'd picked up a box containing a new bike for Robby's Christmas present. She only needed to assemble it to have it ready for him when he awoke Christmas morning.

A car stopped at the curb as she was struggling to get a grip on the oversize box. She turned and saw Jake get out of the car and approach her. His injuries from their fight for survival were still evident—the sling on his arm, the limp in his step from the knife wound to his leg, and the bruises and cuts on his face from the car wreck and beatings. It was a wonder to her that he was still standing.

"Need some help with that?" he asked.

She nodded. "Thanks. It's a little awkward for me but can you handle it?"

He lifted the box from the trunk with little difficulty. She closed the trunk and motioned to the garage. "Carry it to the garage."

He walked up the driveway and set it down on the garage floor. "A new bike? I'm sure Robby will love it."

"He's been wanting one for a while now. He thinks his tricycle is for babies and wants a big kid bike. Of course he'll still have training wheels for a while."

"Do you need some help assembling it?"

She smiled. "That would be nice but I was going to wait until he'd gone to bed to start. I don't want him running to the back door and seeing pieces scattered around."

"Makes sense. Where is he now?"

"Mom has him occupied decorating Christmas cookies."

He nodded. "That's nice."

This would be the first Christmas that father and son would be together and she realized how special that was. "Do you want to see him?"

He nodded. "Of course, I do. I never want to leave him again." He reached for her hand and she took his. "I never want to leave either of you again."

She closed the distance between them and kissed him. "And you never have to, Jake."

"I went shopping this afternoon and got Robby some presents. They're in the car. But I have something for you too." He reached into his pocket and pulled out a ring and held it out to her.

Her heart raced as he reached for her hand. She stared up into his eyes and saw everything she wanted out of life.

"Sabrina Reagan, will you make me the happiest man alive and be my wife?"

Tears of happiness filled her eyes. She'd loved Jake for so many years and knew she would love him for the rest of her life. The decision was an easy one but she still hesitated to say yes. "I want to marry you, Jake. Only, are you sure you can forgive me for not telling you about Robby?"

He waved away those concerns. "I want a future with you and my son and that means moving forward not looking backward. Besides, I'm the one who needs your forgiveness. I should never have left you five years ago. I regret it so much and every day since. Max told me I was a fool for letting you go but I couldn't stand by and watch you destroy yourself. I'm so sorry. I promise you here and now that I will never leave you again. Never. Don't ever doubt that."

His assurances were just the balm she needed to get past her worries. She would never doubt him again and never push him away. "I won't."

He smiled as he slipped the ring on her finger then pulled her to him for a long kiss to seal their future together.

"Does this mean you're moving back to Mercy?" she asked him. They hadn't discussed it and she was willing to go wherever he wanted, but she needn't have worried.

"Absolutely," he assured her. "Where else would I live? This is where my family is."

She was certain Kent would offer him a position at the sheriff's office but they could work all that out later. All that mattered now was that they were together and would always be.

She clasped his hand in hers. "Let's go inside and give our son the news that we're going to be a family." They walked hand in hand into the house to give Robby the best Christmas possible.

* * * * *

Dear Reader,

I hope you enjoyed getting to know Jake and Sabrina and all the members of the Mercy County Sheriff's Office. You'll be seeing them again in the next books.

Jake and Sabrina got what we all long for—a second chance to make things right. I love writing second chance stories because without the opportunity to prove that we've learned from our mistakes, life would be a very unpleasant place. Thank goodness Jesus has never denied us second chances.

Join me as I continue through this new series and get to know these Lone Star defenders.

I love hearing from my readers. You can reach me online through my website www.virginiavaughanonline.com or on Facebook at www.facebook.com/

ginvaughanbooks. You can also reach out to me through the publisher.

Til next time, happy reading!
Virginia